The Wrong Man

To Liam

THE
WRONG

DANNY MORRISON

MAN

A NOVEL

ROBERTS RINEHART PUBLISHERS

Published in the U.S. and Canada by Roberts Rinehart Publishers
6309 Monarch Park Place, Niwot, Colorado 80503
TEL 303.530.4400

Distributed to the trade in the U.S. and Canada by
Publishers Group West

First published in Ireland in 1996 by Mercier Press
Copyright © 1997 Danny Morrison

10 9 8 7 6 5 4 3 2 1
Library of Congress Catalog Card Number 97-67698
ISBN 1-57098-102-7

The Wrong Man is a work of fiction. All the characters and situations in the book are entirely imaginary and bear no relation to any real person or actual happenings.

Cover design: Ann W. Douden
Typesetting: Red Barn Publishing, Skeagh, Skibbereen, Co. Cork, Ireland

Cover photograph © Colman Doyle

Printed in the United States of America

Prologue

TOD SNORTED SEVERAL TIMES until he was startled into a vague state of consciousness, drowsily not knowing whether this was his own bed or if it were day or night outside, except that he felt concussed and still drunk. His neck was sore and he could flex it only through ratchets of movement.

As he looked down, an image appeared – a small patch of floral pattern on a carpet. He realized he was seeing out of one eye, which had a limited scope. The other, his left, injured in a baton charge weeks earlier, was throbbing again and felt as if it were about to explode. When he attempted to rub his eyes his arms wouldn't work and he began to panic. He tried to let out a scream for Sal to come to his aid only to realize that his jaw was already prised open and something swollen filled his mouth. He shook his body and felt the clothesline bite into his chest, wrists and ankles.

Then he realized that he was sitting upright in a chair and that he was hooded. He curled his toes: he was without socks or shoes.

Suddenly, the previous night became connected to the present, his heart shrank with fear and his pulse raced, resounding in his ears. He had an overwhelming desire to crawl back into the safety of his mother's womb, or be born again in another country in another time with another chance.

He tried to piece together the night's events.

He remembered borrowing money from Sal at home, losing most of it on the gaming machine in the pub, winning it and more back. Someone had suggested they go to a dance in Ardoyne. He didn't even bother to ring Sal. He regretted that now. Sal. Sal and Nuala.

They had piled into taxis. He remembered drinking Harvey Wallbangers in the club; dancing and showing off as a circle of women handclapped him; the flashing lights; falling on the floor of the toilets, someone pulling his trousers up and buckling them. Everyone laughing. At the back of the hall he kissed a girl, perhaps two girls. More laughter. There was talk of getting another taxi, going to a party in the New Lodge or Turf Lodge. It was all hazy but he recalled the blast of fresh air on his face and a car and a drive and a fight and darkness. Or was the fight before he got into the car with the girl he'd been chatting up? He wasn't sure . . . he wasn't sure. He couldn't remember if at that stage she was still with him or had got into another car.

He tried to listen but could hear nothing in the bedroom except his own breathing and the rumblings of his insides. He imagined that the room was bare and he alone. His sore neck had thawed a little, allowing him to tilt his head back more freely and find the gap in the hood. He moved his eye along the carpet. To his right a newspaper was spread out. On it were a screwdriver, a claw hammer and carpenter nails.

He thought he might be in the custody of the IRA. He tilted his head back further and then noticed a pair of pliers and the blades of a long boning knife and a skinner.

"The IRA bastard's awake," said a squeaky voice.

"Is he now. Welcome to the Shankill, you fenian cunt." The voice of the second man sounded husky, like that of a heavy smoker whose phlegmy throat thickly coats each word.

Tod's chest heaved and convulsed a few times. He'd been through so much fear and confusion over the past four or five weeks, enough to drive anyone insane, and he didn't think he could take any more. He tried to gather his wits about him, to think a way out, but the sheer terror of his predicament transfixed his thoughts. He burst into a flood of tears and found some solace in their childish expression – the implicit homage to forces adult, the bid for favor and sympathy.

"I'm going to laugh my bollocks clean off if this cunt keeps this up!" said the second man, slapping Tod's thigh jovially. "Get it out of you, son! Get it out! Say your fucking Hail Marys because tonight you'll be in heaven."

"Aye, after I put you through hell!" said the first man.

A laugh from the corner indicated the presence of a third.

Tod sobbed, long and droning. Mucus soon congested his nose and he had great difficulty in getting enough air. His lungs began to drown in an asthmatic attack and he tried to gasp and shook his head from side to side in panic.

"Maloney's going to kill himself, boys, if he doesn't settle."

He felt as if his captors were scrutinizing him from just inches away.

"You're fucking spot on there. He's ready to pass out."

"He's going to asphyxiate himself," said the voice from the corner which had an eerie, even tenor.

"Uhhh, me Dumbo Orangeman. Me dunno what ficksey ate mean, Boss. Me dumb Orange bastard . . . Isn't that so, you fenian cunt," said the squeaky voice. He slapped Tod across the ear, causing a small explosion inside his head.

Tod's lungs were screaming for air, his chest in agony, and his head creaked on ligatures like eroded ballbearings inside his neck. Someone was spraying his asthma inhaler around the room and laughing.

"Know what I'd love to try?" said his assailant, addressing the gang.

"What's that, Sammy?" said Husky.

"If you could take the door off a microwave . . ."

"Right . . ."

"And still get it to work . . ."

"Right . . ."

"You could watch his foot cook!"

"Sammy, wise-to-fuck up! The waves would get out and bounce all over the fucking place. We'd be walking around the Shankill like two Pakis."

"Just you stick to amputations," said the one Tod took to be Boss, their leader. "Go ahead. Take off his big toe."

Tod felt his foot being gripped and the blade of a knife begin to break the cushion of flesh around the bone of his toe. He jerked as if a million volts had been passed through his body.

"Hold it. Hold it. He's trying to tell you something," said Husky.

"It's okay, boy, it's only the knife, not the micro."

"Seriously, he's trying to tell you something . . ."

"Naw. He'll only scream if we take out the sock."

Tod shook his head vigorously, begging them to trust him. He felt a hand partly lift the hood, a hand with the iron smell of blood and freshly-smoked cigarette on it. The sock was pulled from his mouth. He drank so much air that he passed out for several seconds. Unconsciousness was an instant of bliss but when he came to he was still in hell.

"I can help you!" he gasped. "I'll do anything for you!"

"Uhh, Dumbo Orangeman, uhhh, speaking, Boss. Uhhh, what does the prisoner mean, uhhh, he'll do anything? Like, resign from the IRA? Ach, that's it all over then. Phone him a taxi, would you, then we'll all sing 'Auld Lang Syne'." Tod was again thumped on the ear. "You fucking IRA bastard, Malone. Eh? What do you fucking take us for? Not in the IRA!"

"I'm not, I swear."

"You fucking are!"

"On my kid's life, I swear," cried Tod.

"Ach, God, his wee baby. Isn't that lovely. You haven't a photo, have you?"

"Is the little orphan a boy or a girl?"

"Listen," said Boss. "Why do you think we picked you? We don't kill just anybody. We know who you are. Our friends in the security forces gave us your name. Thomas 'Tod' Malone, aged twenty-one, and a key player. Once charged with hijacking and IRA membership. Charges withdrawn."

"I swear to God, that's not me. It's a mistake! It's a mistake! That's my brother. I fucking swear on the life of my child, that's my brother."

"This child gets around, boys, doesn't it?" he said with a laugh.

"Tod, Tod, my man. You're going to all this bother for nothing. We've a photo of you taken by the Royal Ulster Constabulary in Castlereagh on 27 April. 8:15 a.m. to be precise. It's you, son. It's you."

As one log sank beneath the hurtling river, Tod leaped to the next.

"That photo's probably of me," he conceded, "but I'm not Tod Malone. A mistake's been made."

"Who are you, then?"

"I'm Richard. Richard Malone, Tod's older brother."

They all laughed.

" . . . a fucking scream, or what!"

"A comedian . . . 'Richard!' Tricky Dicky. Did you ever!"

"Tod. You have no brother. Isn't that so? . . . Tod? . . . Tod?"

"What?" he said, subdued.

"Why are you telling us lies?"

"Because I'm afraid and I don't want to die."

"Reasonable enough answer. Are you going to start telling us the truth?"

"Yes."

"Do you know where you are?"

"No."

"Do you know who we are?"

"The UVF or the IRA."

"The UVF or the IRA? Why do you say that?"

"You might be pretending to be the UVF to see if I'll squeal on the IRA. It's an old trick."

"Now, that's a complicated one," continued Boss. "But it does suggest the IRA thinks there's some merit in lifting you and that you've got something to hide. Or that you've got some valuable information to give. Doesn't it?"

He couldn't answer.

"Tell you what, Tod," said Boss, lifting the hood a little and violently shoving the sock back into his mouth. "Tell you what . . . Sammy . . . Sammy. Take this lying Provo over behind the wasteground and put two in his handsome looks. He'll know who we are then."

Tod struggled in the chair, bewildered, like a lobster suddenly plunged into the shock of a boiling pot.

"What about the microwave first?"

"Just put two in his face, Sammy. This person does not recognize some Christian charity when it's being shown."

Tod again shook his head vigorously.

"For God's sake I've to pick the kids up from school, what is it now? . . . Take the sock out, Sammy," said Boss.

"You take it out, he might have something."

"No, you take it out, I'm a staff officer."

"It would be fucking quicker shooting him."

"Sammy? Sammmmeeeee?"

"It's okay, Boss, I'll fucking take it out," said the other one, and as he wrenched the sock from Tod's mouth it caught on his front teeth, whiplashing his head.

"I'm an IRA informer!" gasped Tod. "Please believe me. I've been working for the police for years. I hate the Provos as much as you. We're on the same side," he sobbed. "Please . . ."

"He's what? What did he say?"

"He says he's working for who?"

"He says he's an informer," said Boss, relaxing.

"Yeah, but he's still a fucking taig."

"Aye, and fucking better looking than us . . . And did you see where his clothes came from . . ."

"I'll do anything," said Tod. "Anything. Please, don't kill me. I've never hurt anybody. I've never shot any Protestants. I hate the IRA, hate them, hate them. They've ruined my life. I'll do anything but please don't kill me. I *am* a police informer. I am, I swear. You've got to believe me. I've been informing on the IRA for years now. Arms dumps. Explosives. Safe houses. I can do the same for you, even more. You can put your hands on the top operators, Raymond Massey, Pat Doyle, the IRA, Sinn Féin, you name them, I can get you them and they'll not know what hit them. I'll help you, I swear. But please don't kill me . . ." Then his voice trailed away, " . . . what's the use . . . what's the use," and he began sobbing.

"Shut-to-fuck up."

"Please give's my spray, I need my spray. Please?"

"Work the spray for him, Sammy," said Boss.

"For *this* cunt?"

"Give it to him," said Boss to Husky.

Tod inhaled as best he could.

"Got enough?" asked Boss.

"Just some more please . . . Thank you."

"Right, Tod. If all the boys and girls are sitting properly we shall begin. What was the first piece of information you gave the security forces?"

"Eh," he said, sniffling, trying to compose himself. "I gave them a rundown of who was who in the organization and what jobs they had carried out. I bugged rifles in Ballymurphy and got two men caught. I put faulty detonators on bombs so that they wouldn't go off. I saved one of your men from being killed, Causland. Told the RUC . . ."

"When was this?"

"Two weeks ago. I phoned my handler, and told him that

a .45 was being moved to Twinbrook. They were gonna do Causland, out by Dunmurry. A girl was caught with the gun down her jeans . . ."

"May have been a coincidence?"

"No, no. It wasn't. It was my call."

"What was her name?"

"Tina Owens."

"Did you get paid for that?"

"Fifty quid. I got fifty quid."

"Don't believe you," said Boss, suddenly losing his temper, a change of mood which shattered Tod's only hope. "Fifty quid! Cut the fucker's throat. He's lying. Cut it now!"

"No, no. Please," cried Tod, blubbering. "Bobby Quinn! Bobby Quinn! Shot dead by the SAS six weeks ago! I gave the information, I gave the information!"

Hardly had the last word been uttered when a man's fist caught Tod under the chin, cracking his jaw and sending him tumbling along with the chair in which he was trussed. This man leaned over and snatched the hood from his head.

"Pat!" exclaimed Tod. "Pat! Pat! Thank God, it's you! Thank God, it's you," and he began crying again as if from relief. His good eye was swimming but when he looked around him he quickly observed that there were five men in the room, not three.

"Who do you think you're kidding," said Pat Doyle. He turned to Raymond Massey.

Raymond still couldn't take it in.

"You shouldn't have hit him, you stupid bastard," said the one nicknamed Boss to Pat. "We would have got everything out of him without putting a finger on him. Now he's seen our faces."

"Does it matter?" said the one with the husky voice. Gerry Kerr from Ardoyne, thought Tod. Gerry Kerr! He had seen him at a dance with Tina Owens, though he had never spoken to him before. Gerry Kerr! A shiver ran down his spine.

Boss scowled at Kerr's remark. "This man's a Volunteer. We need to hear his side of it. Are you listening, Malone?"

Raymond bent down and righted Tod in his chair.

"Raymond," whispered Tod, in a broken but calm voice. "That was all lies. It was all lies, I swear. I didn't squeal on Bobby. Please believe me. I only said that because I thought you were loyalists and I wanted to save my life. But I didn't get Bobby killed, honestly."

" 'Honestly?' You're a slug," said Pat. "A low-life."

"My throat's parched. I need a sip of water. Honestly. I can't talk without it and I think my jaw's broken."

"It's a pity you weren't born with a broken jaw," said Pat. "Big Bobby would still be alive, Tina wouldn't be in jail and fuck knows how many operations would have gone ahead."

"I swear on the soul of my child, I never got Bobby killed nor Tina arrested. That was all lies I told. I swear."

"Pretty convincing lies."

"No! It's the truth. The truth. I didn't know about that job. I wasn't at the meeting that planned it. Raymond, I was sick that week. Remember? I was out of it. And Ballymurphy? When was I ever in Ballymurphy with rifles? Never! And bum detonators? Sure I never made up a bomb. You know that."

"Tod, do you think I'm a fool? A minute ago you were offering up Raymie and me to the UVF on a plate. Isn't that true?"

"Pat, I was afraid."

"Nothing but the wrong price would have prevented you from setting us up," he persisted.

"No. I wouldn't have done that! Listen. After Bobby's death, you, Raymond and I did the hotel, didn't we! And you, Pat, you and I did the booby-trap which injured the Brits, and you weren't caught, were you!"

"Proves nothing," said Pat. "The Branch were letting you maintain your credibility or else you didn't tell them in case they'd dirty-joe you . . ."

"Fuck's sake, lads! Is this it? An answer for everything?"

"We'll ask the questions," said Boss. "And you'll supply the answers. You must know this yourself, Tod, that touts don't give to the Branch everything they know. It makes them think they've some control. Some don't even accept money. It gives them a sense of honor, that they're not corrupt. So, because all the operations that you knew about, or were on, weren't passed on to the Brits doesn't mean you're innocent."

"I haven't a chance, have I? Kuhh. Kuhh. My throat's dry. Water, please. Some water."

"I'll get some," said Raymond. He returned after a minute, during which time no one in the room spoke to Tod. "Open." He gave Tod two or three gulps.

"Thanks, Raymie. Can I go to the toilet?"

"What do you say?" said Squeaky.

"Please."

"No."

"But I need to . . . badly . . ."

"Nobody's stopping you," said Kerr.

"Please, Raymie? Raymond, I'm desperate. It's running out of me."

"Fuck, but you're one repulsive person. I don't know what any woman ever saw in you," said Pat.

"Please, lads. I'm dying."

"I'll take him," said Raymond, finally.

"Will you be okay with him? You won't strangle him in there?" said Boss, drolly.

"If he's proved guilty, Tod knows what I'll do. Don't you, Tod?"

Tod said nothing.

"Okay, but keep his hands tied."

He was released from the chair, unsteady on his feet.

Raymond put down the toilet seat, turned to Tod, unbuckled his trousers and rolled down his underpants.

"Thanks," said Tod.

As soon as Tod sat on the toilet the diarrhea gushed out of him.

Raymond looked away, looked into a mirror above the hand-basin, looked up at the light bulb hanging from the ceiling.

"Raymond, what's all this about? I am really, really afraid I'll admit to something I haven't done. It's not like being in Castlereagh with the police or anything like it. Will you help me? Look after me. For Sal and Nuala's sake, if there's anything you can do for me please help me."

"Tod. You tried to get me killed."

"No, Raymie. No. No. It's just not true."

"But why did you squeal on Tina? She was your comrade. Your friend."

"I didn't! Won't somebody believe me!"

"Tod. Why did you do it? Why?"

Tod burst into tears. "I've no right to ask, Raymond, but help me, please help me."

"Are you finished in there?" shouted Boss.

"Coming now," said Raymond. He cleaned up Tod, then pulled up his underpants.

"Thanks. Raymie, you will help me, won't you?"

Raymond washed his hands. "Let's get back."

"Just a second. Just a second."

"Tod. Stop stalling. Let's get it over with."

"But you believe me, don't you, Raymond?"

"There's evidence."

"What evidence? There's no evidence."

"You'll hear. You'll know soon enough."

When they were coming out of the bathroom Pat stopped in front of them. "Stay there. There's a problem."

"What's the problem?" asked Raymond.

"Someone's downstairs. Your man's talking to him now. We might have to leave. There's heavy searching and this house isn't the safest."

Tod became suspicious.

Boss came up the stairs. "Bring him back into the bedroom," he said, nodding. They returned and closed the door and Tod was put back in the chair.

"Tod, we're moving you, okay?"

"Where are you taking me! You're not gonna shoot me, are you? Are you!" His voice was shaking.

"Tod, fuck up. We haven't even spoken to you yet. We're walking you to another house where there's a car to pick us up. We'll continue the debriefing later."

"What's gonna happen over there? What's next?"

"I told you before. We'll ask the questions. Over there we'll continue with the debriefing."

"I'm going to the border. I'm dead, amn't I?"

"Not necessarily," said Boss. "You might come up with an explanation that stuns us all."

"Though I've never heard one yet," laughed Squeaky.

Boss looked at Squeaky with displeasure and shook his head. He had wanted Tod calm to make the removal simple.

"No shoes," said Boss. Boss sent Squeaky out to scout the area. "He'll be back in a minute. Get ready."

"I'm being shot now, amn't I, Raymond?" said Tod, quivering.

"You're not, Tod," replied Raymond. "You know the rules. You're a Volunteer. You'll be courtmartialled and then it's up to the army leadership. Look, it's me that'll be taking you out the back and across the street. Don't mess about and everything will be okay. Trust me."

"I'll be with you the whole way?"

"You'll be with me. We'll have to put the sock in."

"If you only knew how innocent I am, if you only knew . . ."

"Now, stand still till I put this back on." He put the sock in, then placed the hood over Tod's head.

"Are we ready?" said Boss. Kerr nodded from the landing, checked the pistol for Raymond and quietly passed it over to him.

He put it down his waistband.

"Are you ready, Tod?" asked Raymond. He expected a nod but instead Tod went into what appeared to be a fit of uncontrollable shaking.

"Calm down, calm down, you'll be all right." Raymond raised the hood a little and pulled out the sock.

"Jesus Christ, Jesus Christ, you're not going to shoot me, are you, Raymond, are you?" he sobbed. "Think of Nuala and Sal. This can't happen, can't happen . . . You've got the wrong man . . ."

"Tod, I've already told you. We just have to go to another house."

"You're sure, Raymond? Are you really really sure? You're not just saying that, are you? You're sure?"

"I'm sure."

"Okay, Raymond. I'll trust you. I'll trust you, I will. You never told me lies before. You're sure, now?"

"I'm sure. I'm putting the sock in now. Take it easy. You'll be okay."

Scumbag, mouthed Kerr at the hooded man. Fucking scumbag. And he raised his hand as if brandishing a gun and shook it at Tod.

1

THE CELL DOOR was unlocked. Staring out through the bars and the broken window with their backs to two warders stood Raymond and Bobby, each draped in a poncho roughly fashioned from a blanket. Like the long beard he sported, the blanket had been a symbol of resistance for four years.

"Come on, let's go," said one.

"Put the towel around you. That's an order," said the other.

Raymond ignored the directive, kissed the ends of his blanket, dropped it in the corner and walked naked towards the door. Bobby said something to Raymond in Irish and they both laughed.

"Look, Massey, you're going home, okay? You've made your point. Now do us a favor and cover yourself with a towel. Otherwise you can't go to the governor's office."

"I'm not wearing it," he said.

Róisín Reynolds was going back to bed. Her ex-husband, Micky, had just picked up their son Aidan and she had fully intended doing the housework. But after they had left she felt so carefree that she returned to bed with a breakfast tray containing a pot of tea, milk in a miniature ceramic ewer, a pot of strawberry jam, two rounds of toast and a bowl of muesli into which she had sliced up half a banana. Propped up on four pillows she could see her reflection in the mirror of the open wardrobe door and smiled. She was at peace with herself, had slowly hugged the world and brought it to her breast.

She ate her fill, set the tray down at the side of the bed and licked her lips.

"*Très bien*, madame," she said aloud.

With the palms of her outstretched hands she flattened the duvet so that her legs were contoured, then she remembered something, kicked off the cover, drew up her knees and ran her hand up and down her shins and calves. Yes, they needed shaving.

She sank back into the feathery matrix her body created and planned her day. Next: bath. An hour-long soak in water so hot it would tan a hide. Every pore would empty itself of its residue of microscopic blemish, leaving her skin pure and smooth. Then she would climb out, wrap herself in her favorite towel and wash her hair using the detachable shower head. She felt the ends of her long blonde hair, some of which were broken, and contemplated getting an inch or two taken off. No need to rush such a decision. Bath! Now! Bath. Her head slowly disappeared below the duvet cover, like a boat going down, except drowning she laughed, pulled the pillows down with her and embraced the surplus of sleep so easily available to the untroubled.

One of the warders returned with his own jerkin.

"Will you wear this?"

Raymond Massey smiled. "Sure."

The other prisoners, locked in their cells, mistook the footsteps for the sound of his release and began banging, cheering and shouting.

He was taken to the governor, listened, bored, to the official speech and was brought back to the wing.

"I want to wash."

"Well, that makes a change."

"Are you sure you remember how?"

They were attempting to be lighthearted.

He showered for ten minutes, came out of the cubicle, approached the mirrors above the sinks and put his face forward for inspection. He ran his fingers through his beard and saw the little white scars around his chin, and on his head a three-inch long cicatrice: battle wounds for refusing to wear a prison uniform, for not moving fast enough on a wing shift, for resisting anal searches.

"Look, you'll not be allowed to walk out of here like that. Will you be reasonable and wear these clothes until you get to reception and pick up your own?"

"I'm not wearing those. It's your problem. After eleven I'm being held illegally."

"You've learnt fuck all, haven't you."

"No! You've learnt fuck all," he said.

A warder came up with an idea and borrowed civilian clothes from two food orderlies. Raymond was lean and tall and looked foolish in the jumper with cuffs inches above his wrists and the trousers into which two of him could have fitted. But they weren't prison clothing and that was what mattered.

He was brought back to his cell. Bobby took a fit of laughing when he saw him.

"What's up?" said Raymond, feigning indignation.

Tears were streaming down Bobby's face. "You should see the look of you!"

"Me? You should see the look of *you*," said Raymond with a smile. "Standing there like a hermit. And that blanket of yours is leaping. You're one dirty baste, Quinn."

They heard the key turning in the lock. The door opened. "Right, Massey, let's have you," said the warder.

"You take care," said Bobby, clasping Raymond.

"You too. And I'll see you in about five months."

"Come on," said the warder. "We haven't got all day."

Raymond shouted down the wing that he was going and from behind their doors they bellowed out a rebel song as his escort took him through the various gates. He felt very strong and proud walking down the yard. He bid loud goodbyes to the prisoners, addressing each by his own name or nickname.

At noon Róisín awoke, leaped out of bed as if she'd just seen a spider, and ran to the bathroom where she turned on the hot tap and scattered in some bubble. Lying in the bath she recommenced her planning, mentally ticking off the few bills she had to pay, and made out her shopping list, which included underpants and socks for her son. She gave herself a thorough soaping – a white flannel for her face and chest, a pink one for her pubic region. Then out of habit, derived from the times when Aidan would suddenly come bursting in to go to the toilet, she placed the flannels over each gleaming, floating breast.

She shaved her legs then lay back and previewed her plans again. What to get Aidan for his birthday? He was a child so easily pleased that the thought of his unselfishness gave her a little glow. He would be as grateful for a comic book as for a bike, unlike the kids of her eldest sister Teresa who at the conclusion of opening all of their many presents would unfailingly declare, "Is that all?" Marie, the youngest, would then cry for more. Róisín was so grateful that Aidan was well-behaved, despite being without a father, except at the weekends when Micky took him away and spoiled him.

She dressed, put on some pale lipstick and walked to the top of the street for a black taxi. On the way into town the taxi slowed and the sound of car horns filled the air. She wondered if there was a British army or police checkpoint somewhere ahead. But this time it was from protestors along the road giving out leaflets and asking drivers to sound their horns in support of the political prisoners. The woman sitting next to Róisín opened her purse, pulled down the window and threw her spare coins into the plastic bucket held up to her. Other passengers, including Róisín, did the same, and wished them luck.

Downtown she wandered the streets and had several long conversations with acquaintances she met, which for her was the best part of shopping. In a second-hand bookshop she picked up a French grammar for fifty pence, a bargain which thoroughly cheered her. She had arranged to meet her sister Lilian in the Castle Inn where they could have a drink and catch up on each other's news until the taxi queues subsided. Lilian tried to persuade her to come out with her and her husband Frank to a dance that night. They could make up a foursome with a friend of Frank. She said she'd see, though she didn't feel like it.

In the car park Raymond's mother and his sister Chrissie threw their arms around him. He was introduced to his widowed mother's friend, Jack, in whose car they were traveling.

That night, Raymond was still not used to his new clothes, which made him itch. He had had his black hair cut and his beard trimmed and had been persuaded to go out for a quiet drink. However, when he stepped into the club's main hall it was decked with bunting welcoming him home and everyone cheered him. He wagged his finger at Chrissie who had arranged everything. He noticed how attractive all the women appeared. After the drab environment of jail the colors of their clothes stood out and their perfumes smelt like wild flowers.

He saw some IRA men whom he knew and went out to the manager's office to speak to them in private and was gone for over an hour. Then he came and sat between his mother and Chrissie, who was with her boyfriend Gerry to whom he had just been introduced.

"It's great to have you back home," said Chrissie, cuddling up to him. "I'm so proud of you. Did I ever tell you about the first time you impressed me?"

"When was that, little sis?" he asked, sipping a pint of

sparkling beer, then licking the condensation from the glass off his fingers like a child.

"Gerry. Gerry, listen to this. I was about eight and Raymond ten. We were in a queue in Grange's shop, beside our school. You don't even remember, Raymond, do you? Just as it was our turn another customer, a man came in. The woman behind the counter ignored us, smiled at the man and asked him what could she get him. You shouted at her, you were almost screaming: 'We were here first. Hey you! We were here first!' She refused to look at you but the man said we were before him. That put her in her place and when she asked us what we wanted you shook the ten-pound note in her face – it was money we'd been given because daddy had just died – took me by the hand and stormed out, telling her to keep her sweets."

Raymond laughed. "I can't remember that at all."

"Do you remember the bath?" asked his mother.

"What was that about?" he said.

"You two in the bath? 'Mammy, Mammy!' Chrissie used to shout. 'Raymond's wee-weed in the bath, I want out! I want out!' 'No, I didn't!' you would cry and to prove it you ducked under the water, took a mouthful and swallowed it!"

"For God's sake, Ma, he doesn't want to hear about that," said Chrissie half-reprovingly, rolling her eyes.

"You're finished, son, aren't you?" whispered his mother, suddenly becoming serious. "You've done your bit, you'll not be going back, isn't that so?"

"Ma!" said Chrissie. "Leave him alone. He's only out and he's not a child."

"I know but I worry. I just want to see you settled, Raymond. You've done your bit. Let some of these others go to jail for a change."

"Nothing's changed, ma, I'm sorry to say."

"Well, we'll not talk about that now," said Chrissie. "Just you enjoy yourself."

Slowly, he got drunk without realizing it and became less tense. He mingled and spoke to the community of old friends in the packed club. He had no recollection of leaving his mother, Jack, aunts and uncles, or traveling in a taxi with Chrissie and Gerry to a party, nor of how he had ended up in bed.

He lifted the duvet and looked at the woman in deep sleep beside him. She was still dressed. He was still in his jeans. Nothing had happened. He shook his head at the thought of how absurd people could be, ensuring that he got drunk and bedded as if it were his right and their duty. Thirty years ago they'd have organized a Mass and a céilí for a prisoner getting released, he thought with amusement. He picked up his shoes and socks, went to the bathroom and showered for the second time in several years. It was heavenly and he shampooed half a dozen times. He was impressed at how easily he was readjusting to the strangeness of clothes after years of nakedness – zipping up his jeans, tucking in a shirt, buttoning the cuffs. He thought it remarkable that his hangover wasn't too bad. He opened the window and every small garden at the back of the houses before him was the source of a thousand forgotten stimuli. He thought of his comrades in jail, staring through bars at wire mesh, day after day, week after week, year after year.

Downstairs, he found Chrissie, a drink in one hand, a cigarette in the other.

"You're up early," he said.

"Early? I haven't been to bed yet." Sitting with her were another young man and girl, who asked Raymond how he felt.

"Great. Great," he replied. "Anybody hear any news?"

"Not another news junkie!" said the girl.

"There's a radio in the living room if you can pick your way over the dead," said the man. "You've missed the nine o'clock. The news is all wired up on a Sunday anyway. Are they going to go ahead with another hunger strike?" he asked.

"Yes, I'm afraid so," said Raymond. Turning to Chrissie, he said, "Where's Gerry?"

"Gerry? Don't talk to me about him! He disappeared during the night, probably back to our flat."

How steady Chrissie was on her feet as they walked up the steep hill, he thought. What a constitution she must have!

"Did you enjoy yourself?" she asked.

"Did I enjoy myself? Did I disgrace myself is more the question."

"No, you didn't," she reassured him. "But you were talking to some girl for ages in the club, a girl called Róisín."

"Róisín? Not Róisín Reynolds? Do you not remember her? I went out with her just before I was arrested."

"Her and who else."

"What was I saying to her?"

"Dunno. I thought she was arguing with you and when I went over you said it was okay."

"I didn't think I was that drunk. I can't even remember that. What did your woman look like?"

"Long, fairly blonde hair. Thin, tallish."

"Shits! That sounds like Róisín okay . . . Oh, I fancied her way back. Then she married. But I heard she got divorced some time ago."

"Keeping tabs then?"

He fended off the remark. "She actually lives in this area," he said. "I hope I didn't say anything to offend her."

"Do you know where she lives? Ha! You do! You have been keeping tabs. I dare you to call in!" said Chrissie.

"She could have somebody in the house."

"So what. I'm with you. And you're only calling in to apologize," she laughed.

"Was it that bad?"

"Sure, how would I know, it was you that was doing the talking. You should have seen the way you left her eye . . ."

"Stop messing me about!"

"Go on, call in. I want to know what you were arguing about."

"I couldn't."

"Lost your balls then," she laughed.

"Okay then. For a dare!"

Róisín rose early, put on her dressing gown and began the cleaning. She vacuumed the stairs and with an open French grammar book in her left hand recited exotic phrases.

Through the hum of the vacuum machine she thought she heard the doorbell ring. She went to the door, opened it and found a man and a woman on her step.

"That's not the same one," Chrissie whispered. "That's not her!"

After a few seconds of embarrassed silence, Róisín suddenly recognized him. "Raymond! God you haven't changed! Come in, come in! When did you get out?"

"Well, I'm off," declared Chrissie in amazement.

Raymond hesitated but let her go.

Before reaching the living room Róisín turned and admired Raymond. Then she gave him a big hug. She was surprised at herself. But it felt so good seeing him.

"Let me see you, let me see you. Your skin's very white and what's this . . . old gray ones in the beard!"

She was tactile with him and he found incredibly sensuous her touching his cheeks and ruffling his hair. She stopped and said she must make him tea or coffee. He followed her to the kitchen, then carried the tray and things to the living room. He sat on the sofa, she in an armchair opposite.

While she spoke he studied her shoulder-length blonde hair which, tucked behind her ears, made a cute bell shape. At her temples the hair was slightly darker. She became aware of him staring and started to laugh, "You're not just here expecting to sleep with me, are you? You prisoners have a wild reputation when you get out." Then she couldn't believe what she had just said.

"Has everything fallen apart since I went to jail? Where have all the morals gone," he joked.

She tried to explain herself. "We get tougher, more cynical, the older we get. I've a son, you know," she said, changing the subject. "Our Aidan. That's his photo . . . over there. A little angel. He's almost five. He's with Micky for the weekend. Micky's remarried, thank God. No longer my responsibility."

"So, what happened?"

"Ach, just weren't right for each other. We saw it early and had the sense to cut our losses. A couple of my aunts said to my mammy: 'She can't get divorced! What'll people think!' But my family gave me their support – they were brilliant."

He was surprised at her assertiveness. When he had first known her she'd been bashful. They dated for several months, on the two or three nights a week when he was free, and he'd eventually persuaded her to sleep with him on New Year's Eve, 1973. Sometimes he missed a date due to his IRA commitments but she never argued, just became sullen. He would try and make it up to her with small presents and surprises which seemingly pleased her. He had been fond of her but she hadn't been his only girlfriend, though she was not to know that. Then, one evening, with difficulty and embarrassment she told him that she'd been asked out by another man, whom she really liked, but didn't want to two-time Raymond. He admired her honesty, a quality which contrasted with his own casual infidelities. He wasn't going to be a hypocrite so he told her to go ahead and was surprised at how upset she became. They had a huge row and he never called back. The other man was Micky. Before Raymond could see her again he was arrested. In jail he had had plenty of time to think over his life, plenty of time to appreciate how he had exploited her and the others for his own gratification.

She let her slippers fall to the ground and tucked her bare

feet under her dressing gown, the movement catching his eye. She asked where he'd been last night.

He told her about the club and the party. "And now here I am."

"Privileged, I'm sure. Did you have a good time?"

"Don't remember."

"You don't remember! Did you die in the earthquake, or what!"

"Well, actually, I did sleep with a girl. Literally. That's all." She raised her eyebrows.

"I swear, nothing happened."

"Expect me to believe that!" she laughed, but from his demeanor felt he was telling the truth.

He shrugged his shoulders and smiled. "Mind if I take off my shoes?"

"Go ahead but do your own darning." She was buoyed by her own animation, as if champagne was going to her head.

He removed his shoes and socks and twiddled his toes. "That's better. I'm not used to those things."

"I'm sure you're not. How long were you on the blanket?"

"From '77 to my release. Four years. And if Bobby Quinn and I hadn't attempted to escape – you remember, Bobby? Yes – we wouldn't have lost political status and we'd have been out three years ago."

"Wasn't very clever, was it, attempting to escape?"

"You know us. Mad republicans. Never give up. We go through mountains, instead of around them. Bobby got a little bit extra but he'll be out this summer for good."

He spotted some books, stood up, crossed the carpeted floor and lifted a paperback.

"*Cousin Bette*. You're into a bit of lechery, I see. There's a character, a woman, can't remember if she's the main character, about whom it is said that if you held her hands she would still find some way of cheating on you with her feet! Of course, it was a man who wrote that and when it comes to women all men are bastards . . . That was the first book I read on remand."

"I know."

"What do you mean?"

"I sent it into you."

"You did?"

"Yes. Then I realized how stupid I was. How unfair to Micky I was being."

"That's incredible! I asked our Chrissie and she didn't know where it came from. Lots of people sent me books."

"Oh yeahhh."

"Well, you know what I mean. Anyway, thank you." He bent down and kissed her.

"You're still not sleeping with me," she laughed, not having felt so bold in a long, long time.

"Aren't we the quare one," he said. "I haven't mentioned it once!"

"That's true, that's true."

"I've changed, you know," he said. "But what have you been doing with yourself, now that you're single?"

"Well, I'm still a mother, don't forget."

"Love life?"

"Love life? Oh, I have a friend whom I see occasionally. And next September I'm going back to college, part-time at first, to do a couple of O-levels this year, some more next year. Then, I'm going to do A-levels. Then, I'm going to go to university and make something of myself!"

"Good for you." He threw his feet up on the sofa and leaned his head back on the scatter cushions. "What subjects?"

"English. French."

"You know, I can't believe I'm lying here. It's incredible. Twenty-four hours ago I was lying in shit, locked up in a bare cell. This is really great, I have to say. Beautiful woman, beautiful house."

"Were you always in solitary confinement or could you ask to share with someone if you were sick or getting it hard?"

He smiled at her naivety. "We were sometimes doubled up. In fact, before I got out, Bobby and I were in a cell together."

She thought about Raymond's lonely years in jail, the things she'd read about prison conditions. She wondered could she have visited him, stuck by him, had they not broken up. She rose from her chair and told him to make room. She took his head on her lap, looked into his eyes, then thought, why not, and kissed his strange lips several times until they both experienced something of the old familiarity. Massaging his temples, she told him to stop frowning. He fell into a light sleep for he didn't know how long and when he awoke she whispered, "Hello."

Outside, the rain beat against the window pane, forming oily beads like glycerine which eventually pedalled down the glass.

"Would you like to go for a walk?" he suddenly asked.

"In *that*?"

"Yeah. It'll be fun. In the park."

"But what about you, you'll get your death. Is that jacket all you've got?"

"For now."

"Okay, you're on. Wait till I get dressed."

The rain had eased off by the time they left the house. In the park she linked him. They sauntered down the deserted tarmac path like an old married couple, around by the bowling club and towards the stone bridge where they stopped to watch the stream now in full spate with a floe of leaves and broken branches. She wanted the whole world to see her. She took him by the collar of his coat and gave him a long kiss. He heard a droning noise. Three army jeeps sped up the path, turned onto the wet lawn and did skids as the soldiers in the observation hatches squealed with delight.

"For Christ's sake, will you look at them bastards!"

"Ignore them, Raymond . . . I said, ignore them!" and she forced his mouth against hers.

Veiled in mist and indistinguishable from the general cloud was the small mountain range behind them – Black Mountain, Divis, Squires Hill, Cave Hill – which ringed the city from west to north. Raymond noticed miles of sky darkening suddenly and realized that torrential rain was charging down the side of the mountain towards them. He opened her umbrella just as thick drops began splattering the fabric and the blustering wind tugged it to one side. Róisín's face was streaked and her eyelashes congealed like tiny oiled feathers. She looked alluring but vulnerable. They waited out the storm under the limited shelter of the trees which occasionally shook and sneezed in the powerful gusts, then they walked home in a sort of calm. Their jeans were saturated, their shoes soaking. She told him to take his off and she gave him pajama bottoms.

She returned from upstairs dressed in leggings and a gansey. She reheated some celery soup she'd had for dinner the night before, gave him back his dried clothes and ushered him out before her son came home.

"To be continued?" he asked.

"To be continued," she smiled. And when she had closed the door behind him she uttered a loud, "Whow-eee!"

2

"IS HE SLEEPING with you?"

"What's this? Sour grapes. Mind your own business, Micky. It's got nothing to do with you."

"That's what you think. I don't want the loyalists breaking in here to kill him, and shooting my son by mistake."

"You're very concerned about your son all of a sudden. It's a pity you weren't thinking about his peace of mind when you were out running around and breaking up this family."

"Oh, here we go round the mulberry bush . . ."

"Get out! I said, get out!"

"You think it was just my fault we broke up and that you had nothing to do with it? All you ever wanted to do was sit in, night after night. You bored me to tears, you've no idea . . ."

"I don't want to hear all this self-justification again. What really gets to you is that I'm doing okay without you. That there's someone in my life other than you. And I'll tell you something, he's ten times better than you."

Micky laughed. "You're pathetic, know that."

"See next week, don't call here. I'll send Aidan over in a taxi. And another thing, stop interrogating him about what goes on in *my* house. And one more thing. Stop buying him things he doesn't need, just to ease your conscience."

"Lover boy'll hardly buy him or you anything."

"Lover boy and Aidan get on too well for your liking, and that's another thing that sticks in your throat."

"Well, I'm telling you, if he's here placing my son's life in danger I'll be on to child welfare, so put that in your pipe," he said, banged the door behind him and joined Aidan, who was waiting in the car.

When Raymond came over later that morning to stay the weekend he could detect that Róisín was not herself. She denied that anything was wrong.

On Sunday morning they were lying in bed. Raymond awoke, then dozed, then awoke again to the mumbled sound of conversations from Mass-goers in the street below the window. He turned to face Róisín. She was staring at the ceiling and clearly had been awake for some time. He asked her what was wrong and then she told him. His first reaction was to tackle Micky but she begged him not to do anything as she didn't want Aidan upset. A few minutes later, Raymond declared, "Micky has a point, you know, about me endangering you and Aidan."

"What do you mean?"

"I'm back in the IRA. It's only fair that you should know."

She sat up in bed and began to cry. "But I thought you were looking for a job. Can't you just go on marches or do political work like the others," she beseeched.

"It's not enough."

"What about Aidan and me?"

"I want us to continue but I don't want to deceive you, either."

"I think you should leave," she said.

"Okay. If that's what you want. I understand." He got up and her heart sank. He was good to Aidan and good for him and most times he was great fun to be with.

"Don't go, Raymond," she said. "Come back to bed."

He got back in.

Around June he moved in with her, but there were times when she could still feel an absence despite the intimacy. When she asked, "What are you thinking?" his replies would be, "How much I hate the Brits and what they've done," or "My comrades. The hunger strikers," or, "The girls in Armagh jail."

"Women," she corrected him. "Women, not girls!"

"Yes," he smiled. "I know they're women. I didn't mean to sound patronizing. When I was on the blanket I called them women. When I was on the blanket my terminology was spot on."

"Women give more than their bodies when they make love," she once said to him as they lay in each other's arms.

"I left part of me behind in jail," he replied. He could be too serious and she saw it her task to dilute his rigorous approach to life with fun and love and affection.

Raymond called into a house in Poleglass to see an IRA runner who would tell the others to meet him at Chrissie's flat the following morning.

He was driving out of the estate when a gang of youths involved in a mêlée spilled from an embankment on to the road in front of him, causing him to brake sharply.

Someone was on the ground being attacked but spinning around and kicking back in a vain attempt to ward off the blows. Then he noticed that another youth was also on the ground being beaten.

Raymond's car negotiated the crowd before pulling in about twenty yards down the road. He leaped from his seat, ran back, and broke into the circle on the road, halting the fight.

"Right, hold it! Hold it! What-to-fuck are yous doing . . . a crowd of yous beating the shite out of two?"

"What's it got to do with you?"

"Yeah, take yourself off, you nosey bastard, or we'll beat the fuck out of you as well," said another, a skinhead.

"Is that right. Was it you said that?"

"Aye. I said it. So fucking what."

"Tell you so fucking what. So fucking what if you and I have a fair dig. Just me and you. That'll sort matters out. Well?"

The gang moved back from Raymond and their two erstwhile victims, one of whom still sat on the ground, his face covered in blood. The other tugged Raymond's arm.

"I was coming from my girlfriend's," he said, "when these hoods jumped the guy walking in front of me. That's how I got sucked in."

"Is that so. Hold on, one sec." Directing his remark at the skinhead, Raymond said, "Hey you. Baldy bollocks. Are you going to fight me or what?"

The skinhead took a run at Raymond, jumped as he approached and landed his boot in Raymond's chest, winding him. Within seconds, the rest of the gang turned their mumblings and grumblings into punches and wild kicks. Raymond headbutted two of them and felt the bones crack around their eyes. He glanced back and forth, dodged, went down on the ground once and bit hard into a leg, causing such a terrifying scream as to instill a general fear. It allowed him a moment to regain his feet.

But Raymond could see that his side was losing. The boy who had spoken to him was pinned to the ground and struggling; the other was being choked and beaten about the head with a cider bottle.

"Right!" shouted Raymond. "Okay! Okay! Yous have won, yous have won!" He kept up the initiative by acting on his words and began dragging the more badly injured youth towards the car, warding off the occasional, humiliating slap. The other youth limped towards the car and opened the driver's door first, then the back. He got in first and helped to pull in the other lad, Raymond lifting in his feet. As Raymond was doing this, someone kicked him dismissively up the backside and laughed. He silently fumed.

While Raymond was getting into the car, the gang members

were cheering and whooping. Raymond took several deep breaths, slowly placed the key in the ignition and turned over the engine like a leisurely gent heading off for a game of Sunday morning golf. He slipped the gearstick into reverse, clutched and slammed the accelerator to the floor. The car shot backwards towards the triumphant gang. Miraculously, the ten or twelve fellas dived hither and thither and Raymond roared like an animal. He braked and put the car in first. As he was revving the engine and speeding in zig-zags towards the gang a brick shattered the windscreen. He slammed on the brakes, the car skidding, hitting the curb and rocking to a halt.

"Mister! Mister! For fuck's sake. We need to get this fella to the Royal. He's fairly fucked. Leave them bastards, leave them."

Raymond reluctantly acceded and punched through the remaining mosaic of windshield as if it were a cobweb. The youth in the back seat took out his inhaler and shook it several times before drawing on the Ventolin.

"Are you okay?" asked Raymond.

"Just about."

"You from up here?"

"No, I'm from down the road."

"What do they call you?"

"Tod Malone."

As they drove to the hospital Raymond questioned him again about what had happened. At the casualty unit the injured youth was put in a wheelchair and Tod limped in behind, followed by Raymond.

"Are you sure you're okay?" asked Raymond.

"Why?" said Tod. "Where are you going?"

"Do you think I'm going to let them get away with that? They're not going to fuck the IRA about. They're not going to fuck ordinary people about. I'm going back up the road. Do you want to come with me?"

"Jesus, no. I'm not up to it. Don't be going back up, you're mad."

"Fucking right I am . . . Come with me, just to watch my back."

"Don't be going. There's too many of them. Aren't you going to get some help?"

"Fucking right I'm going to get help. Are you going to come along?"

"Okay, then," said Tod, relishing the idea of being on the side of the IRA.

Raymond quickly knocked out the remaining glass before driving to his mother's. He ran down the alley at the side of the unlit house and out to the hut at the back. He found the light switch and began scattering the contents of the hut until he found what he was looking for.

In the car Tod shivered and said, "I thought you were going to get help."

"That's what I have got."

"Fellas with guns, I mean?"

"We'll not have time. There's an unsolved rape up in this area and there've been burglaries of old age pensioners. There was also a hit-and-run involving a stolen car which left a wee girl crippled. I bet you, I bet you, some of these bastards were involved in some of those incidents. I brought you one," he said, handing his companion a sewer rod.

He parked his car on one side of the estate and they climbed over a fence and took to the fields. They came to a small hill. Moonlight illuminated the expanse they had to cross so they took the long way around and kept to the hedges which led to the first row of houses. The garden of the last house in the row was enclosed by a small wall. On this wall, below a tall street lamp, at the junction with the main road, the gang members rollicked and drank. Tod heard them laughing and still boasting about their rout. There were about ten of them, but two were girls who hadn't been there earlier.

The skinhead was necking with one of the girls, who was giggling. Raymond crept up behind this couple.

Tod watched, not really knowing what to expect, but excited and afraid. Beside him Raymond rose like some sea monster coming up for air, except his face was that of a warrior and the sewer rod was raised high above his head like a broadsword. With full force he brought it down dead center across his enemy's head, splitting it open. The man fell off the wall and crumpled to the ground. The others were speechless for a second, failing to comprehend what was happening until Raymond came over the wall like a freak wave.

"Want a fucking fight, do you! Want a fucking fight!" he screamed. He began swinging the rod, taking the legs from under two of the youths who hit the ground, elbows first. A cider bottle went whistling past his ear. Somebody slashed him with a knife, and he screamed, "You bastard! You bastard!" He shoved the rod into his assailant's face, trying to gouge out an eye. One attacker managed to circle him and seized him from behind but couldn't budge him. Tod jumped over the wall and whipped the assailant off. Raymond caught the teenager by his hair, forced his nose down and sandpapered it along the ground for several inches before kicking him in the face.

The girls were screaming hysterically, the other youths took fright and began to scatter but he gave chase to the last two, followed by Tod, pursuing them down a twisting street. The youths realized what was happening and split up. But Raymond gained on one, lunged out and clipped his ear, tearing off an earring. The youth stumbled and fell, burst into tears and cried, "Mister, I'm sorry! I'm sorry!"

Raymond turned and saw the other take refuge up the side of a house. He galloped after him but his prey had disappeared into the back garden. Tod was shouting for Raymond to come back before the soldiers or police came on the scene. Raymond was still mad and ran down the path. He approached the coal shed, opened it, took possession of a head of hair from the pit of darkness and dragged the crying fugitive out onto the crazy paving, only to see that the moonlit face was that of a thirteen-

or fourteen-year-old boy. Tod watched in disbelief as Raymond mercilessly raised the rod above his head and the boy cowered. He kept the rod poised until the boy looked up and saw that he was meant to escape. He jumped up and ran.

Sirens could now be heard in the distance. Raymond and Tod climbed over a fence, ran across the field and after a few minutes regained the car.

Raymond switched on the courtesy light and looked in the mirror. There were red smears on his face, his lips were gleaming, and above the corners of his mouth but beyond the reach of his tongue were tiny divots of skin and hair.

"Fuck, that was some fight, mister," said Tod euphorically. "That was some fight!"

"Raymond. You can call me Raymond," he said, as he started the car and they moved off.

"Can I ask you something?"

"Go ahead. What is it?"

"Could you get me into the IRA?"

Raymond laughed. "What age are you?"

"I'm eighteen."

"Why are you only thinking about it now?"

"I did before but some of the IRA guys round our way would put you off, the way they think they are somebody."

"Maybe they are."

"Yeah, but you know what I mean."

"I know what you mean."

"I go to all the marches and riots at night. I want to do more. I hate the Brits and what they've done. They killed a cousin of mine. Out minding his own business. Stopped and searched. Told him he could go on. It was pouring rain, and when he ran away they shot him in the back and said they thought he was going for a gun. You should see my Aunty, she never leaves the house. Has never got over it."

"Well, she's not the only one. There are hundreds like her. And on all sides," said Raymond. "Are you working?"

"Why? Would I have to leave?"

"No, not unless you wanted to."

"If to join the IRA I have to leave work, I will. I work in my uncle's. Owns an electrical shop. But I can't stand by while men are dying on hunger strike. It just brings everything into focus, doesn't it? Were you ever in jail?"

"I was there for seven years and got out four or five months ago."

"What was it like?"

Raymond could imagine Tod's eyes dilate in the darkness of the car, that same eager expression he once had when he begged a man now dead to get him into the IRA. And he did what his predecessor did.

"What's your name again?"

"Thomas. Thomas Malone, though my mates call me Tod."

"Well, Tod, it might seem glamorous but war is a very dirty game and jail, where most people end up, breaks a hell of a lot of them – "

" – It didn't break you. Hasn't broken the hunger strikers –"

"Yes, but we're talking about very special people there. Anyway, you stay out of the IRA. It ruins your life. It ends up owning you."

Tod was offended. "Look, I want to join the IRA. I've thought about it for ages."

"Tod, there's a queue a mile long. Everybody wants to join because of the emotions stirred by the jail. But the IRA has to be careful. There's probably a lot of Brit agents among that queue. Besides, the IRA doesn't need that many people, just dedicated people."

"Would you let me prove myself?"

"How?"

"I'll think of something."

"I'm sure you will," said Raymond, glancing at Tod and seeing something of himself. "Are you any good at babysitting?"

"Babysitting?"

A short distance into the park the noise of traffic on the road below blended into a rumbling silence. The lamplight fell away, creating a pastoral illusion of open fields below stars on this July night. The hunger strike was into its fifth month and six prisoners had already died. Earlier that day Raymond had been released from police custody having been questioned about aiding the escape of IRA men who'd shot their way out of Belfast prison. He hadn't spoken or eaten during the seven days he had been detained.

Róisín pulled off her pumps, ran on tiptoe and disappeared behind several huge oaks.

"Come and get me!" she shouted. But when Raymond followed her he could find no trace. "Over here!" she called from a different direction. He ran as fast as he could and behind a bush he found a pair of discarded jeans and laughed. He scanned the grove and glimpsed a half-naked body dash between two chestnut trees. "She's mad."

This time he caught up with her and seized her around her thin waist. She yelled with delight, turned and ripped open her denim shirt along its studs, acting the hussy. She took him by the hand and they lay down on a mattress of grass scattered with suncrisp haylings which was both cool and warm, soft and itchy.

"Tell me you love me, Mister Raymond Massey," she said, throatily.

"You're drunk," he laughed. "Three glasses of wine and you're blocked! Incredible!"

She clouted him on the head playfully. "Tell me you love me. Go on. Say it."

In his rules to have made such a declaration would have compelled him to follow through.

"I could say it and wouldn't mean it – and you wouldn't want me to do that, would you now, just to get your knickers off?"

"Just to get my knickers off? No problem! They're off. Look!

They're off!" And she threw them away. "Okay, okay, okay, okay. Shush. Don't say anything. Let's not lose the moment. Kiss me!" she demanded. "Not like that! . . . You kiss in small packets and then you stop. Kiss like this . . ." and she forced open his lips and sustained the exchange. She was an amazing teacher. Once, in bed, she had opened his lips and squirted into his mouth tiny refreshing grapes which turned out to be sips of cold water from a bedside glass unnoticed in the dark.

"Watch nobody sees us," he said, nervously.

"Nobody'll see us!" she insisted, and got him to make love. They rolled over several times until they were dizzy. Afterwards, he retrieved their discarded clothes and they dressed. But instead of leaving they lay down again and stared at the heavens.

"Do you remember the last time we were here?" said Róisín.

"The day after I got out."

"You wouldn't think it's almost five months ago. I wonder if we had met earlier than we first did and had married," she said, "how much different our lives would have been? Would you have still been arrested when you were . . ."

" . . . or dead by now."

"Don't say that, Raymond. You know how annoyed I get."

"But it's true."

"Don't be teasing fate. Anyway, do you love me?" she said, pretending to be coy.

He laughed at her.

"You know I'm jealous of your past," she admitted. "Who went with you before me, the music that reminds you of good times and happiness with someone else . . ."

There had been no one else, really, just those few casual acquaintances, none of whom had measured up to Róisín. He smiled again at the sincerity of her probing.

"Oh! You've got secrets!" she said, good-humoredly and he shook his head, No.

Love never survived scrutiny, he believed. It absolutely fell apart because of the things you would never see eye-to-eye on. The fact that she hated your snoring or eating habits and you her mother. The conflicting chemistries. People could never, ever, understand each other, plumb the other's true thoughts, beliefs and motives. They could only make readings: flawed, often deluded interpretations. When romantic love seemed a success it was simply a powerful illusion. In a way, he had come close to love in jail – it was true, that they, the prisoners, were more than blanketmen, they were *brothers*.

He had felt the same about those with whom he had been in action, when four or five lives and his own were fused into one organism, not just in the temporary heat of riding around in a car with rifles or planting a bomb but for days on end experiencing tension, fear and terror; the swarming bacteria of death in one's mouth; then relief, the euphoria of success and the sweetness of survival. And, of course, those comrades who had died he loved with a fierce pride and loyalty, and carried something of them within. Continuity. Survivors carried the dead within, part of the aggregate of responsibility, an eternal compact.

He knew he could destroy Róisín, because as well as throwing her lot in with him, she would be throwing her lot in with him and his principles, his republicanism, which came before him and therefore came before her. But as they had grown in intimacy he had felt something of what she had once said about love-making being more than physical. Intimacy was a strange and mysterious force, and for that very reason needed check. Yet he longed for someone to really understand him and she appeared to do so, could read his moods, could make him smile and rise above his worries. He knew she was a *good* person. And the romantic in her often fired surprising little joys within him.

"Loves you," he whispered carelessly, then terrified in the wake of giving into weakness.

"Too bad!" she laughed. "I was only joking!"

"You're a basket."

"And you're great fun. Loves you too."

He was feeling good. Her companionship. The beer. The sex. The night. "And is that all there was to it? Jesus, that was simple."

"It's enough for now."

"You don't trust me, do you?"

"I don't know what you want," she said.

"I want peace . . . I might even want to get married, for all you know," he said with a smile. "I wouldn't mind kids at some stage."

"Now who's drunk and talking nonsense!"

"It's true. I think," he said.

"Oh yeah, you and me in a little girl? Our own son?"

The notion tickled him. "That's not a bad idea."

"And what about my studies?"

" . . . I'd forgotten about that . . . You're right. It wouldn't be fair. I told you our lives were incompatible!"

"What's that smell?" asked Tod when they lay down together on Róisín's living room floor.

Sal O'Rawe blushed a little. "Lemon shampoo," she said. "I don't think I'll use it again, it's not that nice."

"No, it's okay. Just very strong."

There had been no shampoo. She had used cheap washing-up liquid. For the past year her home had started to crumble, her embittered mother retreating into an armchair by the fireside, that throne from where she denounced her runaway husband. Some days Sal's mother would have a burst of energy, would clean and shop before being overtaken by even longer periods of laziness.

"Just a sec, Thomas," said Sal. "The bathroom."

"I was just getting comfy," said Tod, feigning alarm. But she was already halfway up the stairs. He removed his jeans and shorts and stroked himself in delicious anticipation.

"Jesus, you took your time," he said, when eventually she returned.

"That's better." She had washed her short brown hair again.

"Oom, that smells really nice," said Tod, as she joined him on the carpet. She adjusted their pillows. The radio played pop music. They began kissing: she was conservative in her passion and he considered himself something of an expert. Under her T-shirt his fingers stroked her stomach then fondled her breasts, which he found always slightly cold to his touch.

Sal loved being with Tod. They had been going out together for four months. One afternoon, when he was off work, he brought her into a betting shop, though girls didn't frequent such places. It was mid-week and he had only one pound to his name. He told her straight that he had lost a lot of money that week gambling. Any other fellah, she thought, would have told a lie or said nothing. He pointed to the blackboard on the wall and asked her to pick out a horse in the next race. Everybody was staring at her. Tod told her not to worry. He explained the prices and she chose a twenty-to-one outsider. With butterflies in her stomach she watched the overhead TV and leaped with joy when her horse won. Everyone cheered her. Several men congratulated her and asked her to pick a horse for them but she was too shy. With the proceeds Tod took her to a pizza parlor that night and bought two bottles of wine. That was her first time drunk; the first time she'd ever eaten olives or even seen them.

She thought Tod was more handsome than any of her previous few boyfriends. Even though he had left school without any exams, had been sacked from a youth employment scheme and now worked with his uncle, he knew about everything, was always doing crosswords and had passed his driving test, he said, before even putting his uncle's car into gear.

This was the third time they were minding Aidan. On that first occasion, when they were alone, Tod told her that Raymond Massey was probably the bravest man in Ireland and she wasn't to breathe a word of it but that he had killed soldiers and policemen, planned prison escapes, raided banks, was an expert in explosives and bomb-making, and knew all the tactics of guerrilla warfare. She had been in awe up until the mention of the word "guerrilla" which made her giggle.

"It's not funny, Sal, so I don't know what you're laughing for. I said guerrilla not *gorilla*, or maybe you don't know the difference."

"I'm sorry, Thomas. I didn't mean any offence."

"That's okay. 'Guerrilla' comes from the name given by Napoleon to those small groups in Spain who harassed his soldiers in some war back in the eighteenth or nineteenth century."

"I see what you mean, now," she said. "How do you spell it?"

"GORILLA."

"But that's . . ." Then she saw him put out his tongue.

It was when they were last babysitting for Róisín and Raymond, two weeks earlier, that Tod told her he was joining the IRA. She said she was afraid but her admiration for him was palpable and he immediately followed up by asking her to make love, for him. Until then she had only gone so far, standing with Tod in the alley at the side of her house, panicking when some neighbor put out ashes or got coal. So that night in Róisín's she let him go all the way. She told him she knew when it was safe. It had been a strange experience. Tod was incredibly grateful and told her that he loved her, the first time any boy had used those words.

She was sixteen and she was a woman.

Reveries on Tod's love for her saw her through domestic misery, the household slovenry, empty toilet roll holder, no clean towel, no milk for breakfast, brothers demanding their shirts be washed and dinners made.

She arched her backside and removed her knickers in that brilliant peeling journey that pleased him so much. He told her he loved watching her do that and he always sighed when he saw this part of her naked, studied her for what seemed like immodestly long before getting on top of her and asking her to put him in.

"Okay, Thomas? Okay?"

"Oh, it's lovely," he whispered. "You've no idea."

After a minute he began to come and repeated, "Oh Sal . . . Oh Sal . . . I love you, I love you . . ."

"I love you too," she said, softly, as he slowed to a halt, then rolled off.

They heard the stairs creak.

"The child!" she gasped.

"Aidan! Stay where you are! I'll be up in a minute. Stay where you are!" he shouted. Tod almost fell over putting on his trousers and they both laughed. Tod found Aidan sitting dutifully on the fourth step of the stairs.

"I'm scared," he said. "I can hear things up in the loft."

"Come on down," said Tod. "Here, climb on my back."

3

"I HOPE WE'RE NOT too late," said Mrs. Massey, tetchily.

"Well, if we are, we know who to blame," said Róisín, referring to Raymond's failing to be on time to mind Aidan, as promised. When he had come in her glare burnt his cheeks. But she made up before leaving, their disputes always being short-lived.

Mrs. Massey told Jack to turn right at the cinema. They drove down a long avenue, passed a health center, turned right again and parked outside an old three-storey house.

"This is Mrs. Reiney's house. I hope Mrs. Haskins hasn't left. You come back in about an hour, Jack."

As they were entering the house two women, oblivious of everything but their intense conversation, were coming out. The new arrivals apologized to Mrs. Reiney for their delay. When they were seated in the parlor and had been served a tray of tea and biscuits Mrs. Massey gave their hostess a long white envelope containing money.

Róisín and Chrissie were giggling and Mrs. Massey glared at them, like a mother at two misbehaving children. Róisín looked around her. The room was tidy but had great potential for dust. The heavy curtains were open but nets of thick denier that choked incoming light hung from an old-fashioned wooden pelmet. The walls had a picture rail and were overadorned with photos and tiny paintings in faded gilt frames. The mantelpiece had an antique clock, set off on either side by trailings of small knick-knacks. What a nightmare to clean, thought Róisín. The suite had broad-fringed armrests, with sofa and chairs draped in antimacassars. Around the room stole two or three cats, rubbing shoulders against the legs of the visitors.

"Who's first, then?" asked Mrs. Reiney, politely.

"I just hope he's sound."

After Bobby saw Jonah's replacement, Tod, he called Raymond into a back bedroom in the small flat. "Jesus Christ, he's dressed all in black like that character out of the Milk Tray advertisement!"

"Never mind that. He's okay, believe me."

"Is he for real?"

"He knows the house and he knows the lay-out. In fact, it's him got us the info."

"Well, I hope it's not a spoof."

"He hasn't been wrong before. Trust me. You're just a bit rusty, with this being your first op back. I was the same."

Despite her reluctance, Róisín was pushed forward by the other two and felt a hint of apprehension although she and Chrissie had been taking it all lightly, as a night away from the gloom of west Belfast. She followed Mrs. Reiney out of the parlor, down a short wainscoted hallway with a dark staircase and stained-glass landing window to the right and into the living room on the left. Mrs. Reiney returned to sit with the others in the parlor and listen for the door.

In the living room a fire had been set in the open grate, but as the August evening was warm it was not kindled. A table was covered in a white lace cloth upon which were doilies neatly arranged and on these cups were belled in their saucers, very genteel. There was a peace about the room or around the presence of the fortune-teller, Mrs. Haskins, who was sipping tea when Róisín entered, but then stopped. She turned over a cup, began pouring for her guest and with a friendly nod intimated for her to take the chair and make herself comfortable.

"You'd be no sugar, yes?"

"That's right," said Róisín. "Well guessed."

Mrs. Haskins smiled. "You are a very pretty girl."

"Woman. I was a girl."

"And why age yourself before your time? Youth is temporary, old age is forever. You should take it as it was meant – a compliment."

"I'm sorry. Thank you, you're right."

"No. Not always right. Just sometimes. So, what would you like to talk about?"

"Me?" said Róisín. "I thought you were the one that was going to do all the talking. Read my palm . . . look at the tea leaves."

The old woman laughed: "Come off it. You don't believe all that, do you?"

"Is this some sort of a take-on? Listen, I've a woman out there in the parlor and if you can't tell her what she had for breakfast and when she's winning the pools she'll go berserk, wreck this house, then this street!"

"We both know that's an exaggeration. This woman, the two of you are related, isn't that so?"

"No."

"Oh. There you go now. But I did say I wasn't always right," she said, with a winsome chuckle.

"That's true, you did say that." Róisín liked the old woman, wasn't really disappointed, didn't mind the easy relaxed flow of conversation in lieu of revelation.

"I see you wear a wedding ring," said Mrs. Haskins.

"Yes, I'm married . . ." said Róisín. She had put on the ring for deception. Then, seeing the puzzled look on the fortune teller's face, she said defiantly, "Do you doubt it? . . . Why, am I a widow or something?"

"Two of you are widows and it is true that your husband is married . . . I'm sorry. Have I upset you?"

"No. Not at all," laughed Róisín.

Mrs. Haskins touched Róisín's finger. "I'm glad I haven't upset you. I only try to help. You see, the ring no longer fits. If you want another one put this old one away. But think long and hard, dear, long and hard, because then you'll stop being a girl. Remember, you couldn't wait to get away from school the first time and I think you'll admit that that was a mistake. Would you like more tea? No? Excuse me while I do." She poured slowly. "How's the figure since you gave up sugar and chocolates?"

"Fine, thanks. No stomach, and the stretch marks aren't too noticea . . ."

"That's big boys for you."

Róisín looked at her.

"You have a boy, I think, who was a big boy. You look like you have a boy."

"Did Mrs. Massey tell you all this? What else did she say?"

"Oh, whoever you are referring to told me nothing, daughter. I have a gift, that's all. Often depends on the sincerity of the person I'm sitting with. And if I can help or suggest an answer I will. I get feelings, some that I can put a meaning to, some that I can't and some that I won't – because the truth isn't always more important than the pain it causes."

"So you know I have a son. Okay, then. How many children will I have?"

"You're a mother of two. There is a father in danger or a dangerous father in their lives . . ."

"Missus," said Róisín, "you're some crack, I have to say! Talking in bloody riddles! I'm not married but divorced. Do you get all your ideas out of magazines and books or what!"

"I can't read," said Mrs. Haskins. "And I can't write."

"I'm sorry, I didn't mean anything by that."

"I know. I know you didn't," said the old woman, as she straightened and massaged her hip. "There's very little evil in you."

"There is no evil in me at all," said Róisín, a little indignantly.

"Oh, there's evil in every one of us, love."

They had to walk only to the edge of the estate, where it bordered a mixed area. Raymond and Tod stealthily led the way, Bobby followed with the holdall, a hundred yards or so behind. It was just after 3 a.m.

Raymond was part of the darkness, melded into the jungle feel of deserted dark streets, understood the wild night sounds threading the atmosphere. A rat went scurrying into a hedge and somewhere distant a dog howled.

Tod, on the other hand, was aware of souls hanging in the air like dew, witnessing all, and he shivered. This was the first time he was going to take part in killing someone and he was aware of its importance, how profound an act it was. Every minute or so he needed to steel himself somewhat but he also found that fascination with the deed itself and his reaction had a momentum outside his will, and he knew that he wanted to follow Raymond Massey everywhere and anywhere because Raymond Massey was so confident that he made you feel invincible and immortal.

When they arrived they waited for Bobby to catch up. They stepped over a small picket gate and went around to the back of the house, watching for discarded toys or anything over which they could stumble. Tod pointed to the kitchen window on a latch. Bobby took from the bag two balaclavas, a rifle and a handgun. Raymond gave Tod a lift on to the sill. He climbed through the window and gingerly placed his feet between glasses grease-stained with fingerprints and plates bearing the remains of rice from a take-away. He slid to the tiled floor, opened the bolts on the back door and emerged. Raymond pointed and Tod knew to go to the garden and watch the street, although he would have preferred to have gone inside with them. At the side of the house Tod used his inhaler and immediately felt his chest relax.

Raymond and Bobby stole through the rooms to the hall before taking stock again, looking anxiously at the top of the landing, from where shots could so easily erupt without warning.

But all was still.

Raymond and Bobby tip-toed up the stairs, turned at the top and listened to the silence. Bobby carried the rifle. He opened the door, stood aside and Raymond rushed in with the shortarm in one hand and a torch in the other.

"Don't move!" he said quietly but with emphasis. The couple in the bed remained as they were, fast asleep, snoring. He crossed the floor and tapped one of the occupants, a balding man in his late thirties, hard on the side of the head with the torch. The man awoke but could see nothing but the blinding light.

"Get out of fucking bed and don't move!"

"What? What's up? What is it?"

"Get out of fucking bed and put your feet on the floor! Where's the gun! Where's your fucking gun?"

"Gun? What gun?"

"Where's your fucking gun! Quickly!"

"Gun? I don't have a gun."

The woman was mumbling, experiencing a nightmare on the hazy border between sleep and consciousness, but she suddenly awoke to a sense of real danger.

"The kids! The kids!" she cried, and before she could be stopped she switched on a bedside lamp. She gasped when she saw the hooded men and the guns and she pulled the sheet up to cover her breasts. The atmosphere of fear suited Raymond.

"You wake the fucking kids," he said, "and we'll shoot you.

Now who's he? . . . Fucking answer me when I ask a question! Who is he?"

"Please don't do anything. Please."

"What did I say? Don't mess about with me!"

"I'm Powderly. Joe Powderly. I'm a Protestant but please don't shoot me."

"What sort of a fucking name is that?" said Bobby.

"He's Joe Powderly. Joe Powderly! He's my boyfriend."

"You're in the UDR, aren't you?" said Bobby.

"Fucking sure I'm not, son. It's a mistake. I swear. Look in my wallet. Joe Powderly, that's me. I'm a TV engineer, a TV engineer. I swear!"

Tod froze when he saw three jeeps turn the corner, the first vehicle slowly scanning the gardens with its spotlight. They went past the house at a crawl, their engines radiating a funereal purr. Then they stopped.

Bobby found the jacket and went through the papers in the wallet. All supported the fact that he was Joseph Powderly. He even had a calling card. Then Bobby came across a membership card for an orange lodge. "Do you walk on the Twelfth?" he asked, revealing no attitude.

"I know what you think. That's old, an old, old card. Look at the year. It's expired. I'm no spy, honest."

"Get down on the fucking floor!" said Raymond. "Down!"

He turned his gun on the woman in case she considered screaming but she had gone mute and was gnawing her knuckles. Powderly got down on the floor. A slight smell of contraceptive rubber rose with the disturbed effluvia of the mattress. Powderly had a paunch and a fat backside which quivered when he fell on the bedroom carpet – as if it were nervous on its own behalf. Human being. On his upper arm was a Union Jack tattoo.

"Hands on head!"

"You're shooting the wrong man, son. I'm just a stupid old engineer, honest. Would I come over to this estate and see Mary

if I was in the UDR. Come off it. For fuck's sake, think about
it."

"You're in the UDR!"

"I'm not, I'm not. I swear. You've the wrong man, the wrong
man . . ."

"Get up!" said Raymond. "Sit on the bed."

Go away, go away, whispered Tod to the jeeps. Please God,
make them go away. He couldn't understand why Raymond
and Bobby were taking so long but he was glad they were.

Powderly pulled the valance over a huge mound of ginger
pubic hair into which his privates had shrivelled. He scratched
his ginger moustache which on one side had been clipped carelessly, leaving a visible patch.

"I'm fucking half drunk, lads. Take it easy with me." He
turned to his lover. "That's the last time we're coming to your
place, Mary," he said, in faltering speech, attempting a joke.
The sides of his mouth were slightly curry-stained. He looked
no more a soldier . . .

"Where are you from?"

"East Belfast."

"Originally?"

"East Belfast."

"Do you know Jackie McKeague?"

"No. Should I?"

"Come on now. Everybody knows Jackie. He did time."

"I swear. I don't know him. I mind my own business, work
at my own wee business."

"How long have you known her?" said Bobby, nodding.

"About seven weeks. Let me think? We met the night of . . .
the night of . . . fuck, I can't remember exactly . . . about seven
weeks." He looked at the woman apologetically.

"How many times have you been over here."

"Here? You mean this part of town? I've been here about
three . . . four times. Isn't that right, Mary?"

She shook her head.

"Do you put up RTE aerials?" asked Raymond, softening.

"Of course I do," laughed Powderly. "I'm not a bigot! Do you want one?"

"Do you think I'd give you my address," joked Raymond. He nodded to Bobby, who now stood relaxed with the muzzle of his rifle pointing at the floor. "Okay. We're leaving you now, Joe. If you phone the cops we'll come back for her and we know where you live. Do you hear me?"

"There's no chance of that lads. No chance. Is there, Mary?" said Powderly. "You boys have a job to do. We'll not be interfering. No way. No way at all."

At last the jeeps moved off and Tod sighed with relief.

Powderly got up with Raymond and Bobby, quickly pulled on underpants, and walked out to the landing as if to bid goodnight to two old drinking companions.

"Hey Joe," said Raymond, cordially. "Don't you be giving us a hard time at them oul checkpoints!"

"I'll wave you through," laughed Powderly before his life loomed before him as having unfairly turned on just a few words.

In an instant Raymond screwed the revolver into Powderly's face and fired twice. Like a bag of bones Powderly doubled and tumbled.

"Find his fucking short!" Raymond shouted to Bobby. "It's here somewhere . . ."

In the car Mrs. Massey was in excellent form: Mrs. Haskins had suggested where at home she should look for misplaced earrings which had belonged to her late mother and which she'd lost months before and been anxious about. She could hardly wait to search.

Róisín invited Mrs. Massey, Chrissie and Jack in but they declined. When she came through the door and found a girl, a total stranger, minding Aidan, who was asleep on the sofa, she had to disguise her anger.

"He said he mightn't be back tonight, Mrs. Massey."

"And who are you, again?"

"I'm Deirdre, Bobby Quinn's sister. He came and got me. They had to go out. I made myself tea, if that's all right?"

"Yes, yes, no problem. How are you going to get home? Is Bobby coming back for you?"

"I'll walk, I'm used to it."

"No, I'll get you a taxi."

"Are you kidding! For that distance! I walk to longer places all the time. Me and my mates walk into town. We once even walked to the zoo . . ."

It wasn't that long ago, thought Róisín, that I would have gone on and on like that myself. She gave the girl a pound and thanked her.

Róisín said goodbye to Deirdre, watched until she got to the corner, giving an enthusiastic wave before disappearing. She stood with her arms crossed, inhaling the fresh night air, then shivered when she thought of those mothers by the bedsides of their dying sons in the H-Blocks. She didn't know how they did it. Such loyalty. Throughout the hunger strike there had been rioting on the main roads almost every night. Tonight it had finished early and there had been no one around when they were returning from the fortune teller.

She looked up at the dark sky which, behind the mountain, glowed with a jaw of light. She was disturbed by anger, at the thought of Raymond running off at the drop of a hat. Then she worried that he might be in danger at that very moment and she shivered again. She tried to console herself with the fact that at least he wasn't out chasing other women. But his devotion and loyalty meant that the damned IRA might as well have been another woman. She had once told Raymond that her break-up with Micky had been because they were incompatible but she suspected that that was something her ex-husband had deceived her into believing and which he had used to justify his unfaithfulness. She had never felt they were unsuited. She had been happy. She'd kept a good home, one to be proud of, gave him a lovely son, pleased him in bed, and still he hadn't been satisfied. She'd thought his jokes about female passersby just that – jokes. She'd been devastated by his leaving. Her poor judgement caused her to doubt herself. Her self-esteem had been eroded to the bone. She winced now when she thought of how she had prostrated herself, biting her tongue, asking him if he needed time to sort himself, that she could be patient. And he took his time too, and she, like a fool, waited whilst he had the best of both worlds, preparing his exit from hers. It had taken her several years to pull the strands of her life back together and then Raymond Massey had reappeared.

Flawed but faithful.

All men are bastards when it comes to women, Raymond had said. And it was true. Well, perhaps true. Not always. No. She recalled lying to Raymond about having a boyfriend that time he got out of jail so that he wouldn't think she'd been left on the shelf: a lie that had compelled her to invent a convincing biography and go through the motions of breaking off the imaginary relationship. That type of silliness made her feel small and pathetic.

She considered locking the front door but decided against. At least Raymond had bathed Aidan and put on his pajamas: that was something. She went to the kitchen, plugged in the kettle, came back to the living room and picked up Aidan, who grumbled angelically in his sleep. After tucking him in bed and kissing him she crossed the landing to her bedroom, undressed and searched for her slip. She pulled back the quilt and burst out laughing. A week before, Raymond had been in Dublin and returned home mid-morning to sleep. She had had to go out without seeing him but underneath the duvet she had laid out at body length a black bra, crotchless knickers, suspenders and black nylons as a tease. Now she found waiting for her on his side of the bed a white vest, a pair of underpants, and winter woolly socks.

What a headcase, she smiled, and went downstairs to get her nightcap of tea.

Later, he slipped naked in beside her. He was chilled and she tutted. She drowsily turned away from him but was really more awake than she pretended.

"I'm sorry, love, but I had to go out. We got word that there was going to be a raid on a house, so Bobby and I had to quickly move the gear to another place." There was that much happening across the city that she was unlikely to put two and two together.

She rolled over, tried to cut him off and said she didn't want to hear.

"Well, if we hadn't moved it the fella would be in the barracks now."

She thought about somebody's husband, some child's father, being spared imprisonment by Raymond's decisiveness. Against her will she was flattered that he had been prepared to confide in her: it brought them that little bit closer. She rolled over to him, rubbed the cold from his arms, squeezed and held his hand.

4

TOD PICKED SAL UP some distance from her mother's. He felt sorry for Mrs. O'Rawe but didn't think she liked him. As for Sal's brothers, he didn't like them. One, Jim, who knew Tod was in the IRA, had asked a favor of him, which had been easy enough to facilitate and this had turned Jim into an ally.

Sal came down the street and smiled when she saw him. But it wasn't her usual sunburst. Tod couldn't accurately describe what it was attracted him to this rather plain girl, except that it was a genuine emotion. She had a heart of gold and he basked in her adoration of him.

He opened the door and she stepped in. She kissed him and they drove off.

"Thomas, I was at the doctor's today."

"And?"

Her hands were joined on her lap and her eyes downcast.

"And!" he said, waiting.

"I'm pregnant."

"Who to?"

She burst into tears.

"Sal! Sal! I was only joking." He pulled in at the side of the Falls Park, and put his arms around her. "I was only kidding you. I thought you had been taking something and couldn't get pregnant."

"I got it all wrong. I'm sorry, Tod. I'm really really sorry. What are we going to do? I hate the house and once I tell my mammy she'll kill me."

"Leave it to me, Sal. Let me worry about it. I'll try and get you somewhere."

"Oh Thomas, I want you to take care of me and I'll always look after you. I will, I swear."

He smiled encouragingly and she thought to herself, how wonderful he is, I'm so lucky.

"It's going to be okay, Sal. You'll see. Let me think about things, okay?"

Later, after dropping her off, he went in search of Raymond to have a talk but couldn't find him. He decided to go for a long drive up the M1 so that he could sort out his thoughts.

There's no way am I abandoning her. No way. He arrived at a simple expedient. I'll get a flat and we'll move in together! His parents would go crazy for a while but they knew how decisive Tod could be. After he'd gone missing once, he told his father straight to his face that he had just returned from a week-long IRA training camp and had the whole issue out with him there and then. His mother had been in tears because all she could see was Tod shot dead like her sister's son. But he had stood his ground and said if they wanted him out he'd go. They relented.

They'll crack up but they'll support me after a bit, he thought, and laughed at the idea of him being a father. Imagine. Me a da!

He drove back to Belfast, bought a bottle of vodka and some beers, drove to Sal's street, got out and knocked on her door.

"Jim. Is your mother in?"

"Is she ever anything else."

"I want to speak to her."

"Come on in."

Sal heard Tod's voice in the hall and came running down-stairs to see what was happening. He had already gone into the living room.

"Mrs. O'Rawe," he said. "You're going to be a granny. Congratulations."

Aidan and two of his cousins were running wild through their Granny Reynolds's living room, banging into furniture, caus-ing a ruckus.

"Aidan!" shouted Róisín. "Slow down!"

"Ach, they're okay. Let them be," said her mother. Róisín, her sisters Lilian and Collette and her mother were having a cup of tea and had done the rounds, enquiring after each other's news.

"So, how's college?" said her mother.

"Still finding my feet but I got good marks for my English essay."

"'Essay?' They were called 'compositions' in my day," said Lilian. "I don't know how you stick at it. I hardly get time to read the paper."

"What's for dinner, today, mammy?" asked Aidan, breath-less.

"Dinner? But sure we had dinner yesterday," said Róisín to the perplexed child, as the four women laughed. "Now, go and get your coat, it doesn't look as if Raymond's coming."

"Mammy, mammy! He's here now! Raymond's here now!"

"Okay," said Róisín to her son, then to her mother: "You'd think he was Santa, the way Aidan gets on."

Raymond came in, car keys jangling from his right hand and sat down on the sofa. "How's the ladies? . . . Mrs. Reynolds . . . Lilian . . . Collette . . . Róisín." They all nodded.

"Raymond," said Mrs. Reynolds. "Would you like a sand-wich or a bit of dinner?"

"No, thanks. I'd something not long ago." He turned to Róisín. "What are we doing? Have you to shop?"

"Yes. Sure you said you'd run me. I've to get for the week."

"No problem. Isn't that why I'm here. At your command. Anywhere you want to go. As long as it takes."

"Perfect man," observed Lilian. "If only they were all like him."

"Oh, listen to Miss Cynical," joked Raymond.

"That rain's not going to go over," said Róisín. "We'd be as well moving now."

When they were in the car he asked Róisín how long she'd been in her mother's.

"Half an hour. I finished college a bit earlier."

"So what were you women talking about?"

"Oh nothing. Nothing that would interest you."

"Is that so?" He turned and threw chewing gum on to Aidan's lap. "Try me," he said.

"Lilian had been joking about us, and my daddy probably not even remembering that I was divorced or that we were living together."

"And what else?"

"Nothing."

"And what else?" he persisted.

"Well, the topic of us came up, how we were getting on, if ever I thought we'd marry."

"And so?" he said.

"So nothing."

"So you don't want to?"

"I didn't say that."

"Then you do."

"I didn't say that either."

"What!"

"Well, not for some time."

"Man is completely confused. Do you or don't you?"

"Are you asking?"

"I didn't say that."

"Are you ruling it out?"

"No. Not at all. We're well suited, so we are."

"And what about the Movement? What about my studies?"

"I can't see the war going on forever. The hunger strike came to an end, didn't it? And why should you stop studying just because you are married?" He wondered why he said that.

Róisín sat back and smiled. Sometimes she felt broody, felt like having another child. Aidan could do with the company. But there was no way she would have a child unless she were married. At other times this reverie would strike her as absolutely crazy, more entrapment. She looked over at Raymond as if she needed to study the product again. Some IRA attacks had caused furious rows between them. She couldn't understand how he could defend many of the things the IRA did. But then when she found herself in the company of critics she sometimes behaved in a similar way.

Raymond could be a very exciting man: there was a depth to him, layers and layers to explore. A richness.

"Of course I'll marry you," she said, as if she had been plainly asked.

"No need to be impetuous," he said.

She looked askance at him.

"Of course we'll get married," he said.

She smiled, hardly believing the subject had been broached and settled so easily.

"Do you mind if we move house?" he said. "A brand new start?"

She liked the house she was in. She had good memories of Aidan's infancy but appreciated how Raymond could feel Micky lurking in the woodwork, the shape of the rooms, the turn on the landing.

"Okay," she said. "That's okay."

An hour later, driving out of the shopping mall, Raymond stopped their car at the main road, to wait for a gap in the traffic. Three jeeps, two army and one RUC, drove past, the observer in the RUC jeep turning his head quickly in recognition. But they were going in opposite directions and Raymond turned on to the road, his indicator automatically knocking itself off when the steering straightened. He drove up Kennedy Way with his windscreen wipers on full when suddenly came the sound of wailing sirens and in his rearview mirror he spotted jeeps with full blazing headlights racing towards him. Two overtook and forced him into the curb.

"What's wrong, Mammy?" Aidan trembled. "What's wrong?"

"Nothing, son. It's okay, it'll be okay."

The police and soldiers alighted, took up various firing positions and several surrounded the car. An RUC officer tapped on the driver's window. Raymond rolled it down.

"License, please."

He handed it over.

"Date of birth."

"It's on the license."

"I'm asking you your date of birth, sir."

"It's on the license."

"For God's sake, give it to him, Raymond," pleaded Róisín.

"It's not the date of birth he wants, love. If I give that, it'll be something else."

"Would you mind stepping out of the vehicle."

Raymond unbuckled his belt, got out and stood in the pouring rain.

"Everybody out," said the officer. "Everybody."

Róisín buttoned up Aidan's duffle, climbed out and fixed her overcoat. The strong gusts had turned the autumn rain into freezing pine needles which flailed her legs. The child huddled against her. On the road another police officer waved through the occasional car, rush-hour not having begun.

Two soldiers thoroughly searched the vehicle. Raymond was asked to open the bonnet and boot. All the shopping, in bags and two medium-sized cardboard boxes, was removed and placed on the streaming road.

"Empty out the contents of your pocket," Raymond was ordered. He set his loose change, keys, a pen, on the roof of the car but offered his banknotes to the policeman.

"Everything on the roof, sir," insisted the officer.

"The money'll blow away. Here, count it, check it."

The policeman stuck his face into Raymond's. "Put the fucking money on the roof!"

Raymond continued holding the money in his hand. The officer seized his arm and twisted it behind his back, forcing him against the body of the car. The money was released and blew across the road.

"Stop that, you!" shouted Róisín. She ran to intervene but was pushed to the ground by a soldier. Aidan began squealing and danced on the spot as if he stood barefoot on hot coals.

"Not such a brave Provo now, Massey, are we!" shouted the officer between clenched teeth. "Tell your fucking ride to shut up, and the bastard!" He pulled Raymond's head back by the hair and shouted, "Ivor! Help me search this piece of shit." Another policeman came and ran his hands up Raymond's legs and grabbed him by the testicles, squeezing them hard and pulling them down, relaxing them, squeezing them again as if he was milking a tit, grinning all the while.

Suddenly, Raymond drew his leg up and kicked this officer on the chin, stunning him. The policeman restraining Raymond forced his arm up into his shoulder blade until a bone snapped and Raymond seemed to die in a blaze of sweat.

"My arm, my arm," he gasped.

"You're under arrest, mister big IRA man, for assaulting a police officer!" He was frogmarched over to a jeep and forced to climb into the back.

The soldiers were summoned, ran from their firing positions and disappeared into their vehicles which then took off. Róisín picked herself up off the ground, burst into tears and clutched Aidan, who was sobbing even more loudly though the danger had passed. She replaced the groceries in the boot but couldn't find the keys. She tried to wave down several cars until the occupants of one, then two, came to her aid.

Sal dabbed her brow with the cuff of her dressing gown, folded away the ironing board and carried the basket of laundry into the bedroom. Before she got there she had to pause. A sharp pain began underneath her toes – or so it seemed. At first she thought a nail had run through her slipper but the pain had no specific location. She set the basket down and placed her hand on the wall to steady herself.

"Oh, I wish Thomas was here," she said. She wasn't due for another week. She became very afraid. She touched herself between her legs and took away a hand gleety with discharge.

"Oh my God! Jesus, Jesus, Jesus! Where's my mammy!"

She broke out in a sweat and bit into her lower lip. She heard a key in the door.

"Thomas! Is that you! Quickly!"

"Yes, it's me! What's up!" He ran up the five steps which led to the landing of their flat. "What's wrong, Sal!"

"I think I'm ready to go."

"But it's too early!"

"I'm in agony."

"Can you walk to the car?"

She was crying like a child. "I don't think I can move. Oh Jesus, Thomas, I think I'm dying. Get my mammy. Phone an ambulance, please. Quickly!"

Sal lay on the hospital bed. She had never been as afraid of anything as she was now. Tod held her hand and repeated the nurse's call for her to push. He felt sorry for Sal, witnessed her agony and told her he loved her. But he still felt a certain detachment from her pain.

Sal was too small and the doctor had to make a cut.

Tod now got caught up in the excitement of the birth and he urged, "Come on! Come on!" as the baby's compressed, gargoyle-like head appeared miraculously through a tiny aperture, turned to face him, then slithered out in a slick of blood and gleet.

"It's a girl, Sal! A wee baby girl!" he exclaimed and looked up only to see that Sal had passed out. Calmly, a nurse put the mask to Sal's face and she came to. Her pale face was wreathed in tears and she smiled weakly.

Whilst Sal rested he telephoned his parents but spoke only to his mother whose congratulations, he felt, could have been more enthusiastic. He had failed to get through to Sal's mother and now left news with a neighbor.

Later, he sat beside Sal as she slept and he wondered what she was dreaming. She looked utterly wrecked, her face puffed, her hair turned scraggy and colorless. Suddenly, she awoke.

"Have you seen her yet?"

"Yes. I saw her when she was born. Don't you remember?"

"Sort of," she said. "What are you doing tonight?"

"Going out to celebrate, of course!"

"Will you be dancing?"

"Listen to you, will I be dancing! Do you not want me to dance?"

"Not really, Thomas, if you don't mind."

"I'll not dance then, okay?"

"Thanks."

Róisín and Raymond were married in a civil wedding at the City Hall. Their reception was in a West Belfast hotel which was staked out by soldiers and police in case any wanted people should be foolish enough to show up.

"Chrissie, Chrissie!" shouted Aidan.

"What is it, big fella?"

"My cousins are throwing stones at the soldiers."

"Where?"

"Outside. Come on to I show you."

Chrissie looked around the room and noticed that all the children were missing. "Sal," she said. "Do you mind coming along with me. The kids have disappeared."

Out in the grounds the soldiers were hiding behind trees as the well-dressed children threw stones which fell short. The soldiers were jumping up and down and squealing as if they were being struck and the kids were laughing. Chrissie and Sal began rounding them up.

"But I want to play rioting with the Brits," complained one child as he was dragged inside.

"Would Róisín not have preferred a church wedding?" asked Bobby, the best man. He, Raymond and Tod were standing at the bar.

"Sure, she's divorced, how could she?" said Tod.

"I know she *couldn't* have, but she still could have *preferred*. Do you understand the difference, Tod?" said Bobby.

"Ach, that," he said.

"It's as well she was divorced," said Raymond. "There's no way would I want to be married in a church. Fuck them."

"I'm not sure about that," said Tod. "I don't fancy that City Hall business myself. Doesn't seem like the real thing . . . Here, who's that honey?"

"Who? Where?"

"Turn and look over towards the loudspeaker on the right. The waitress in the short black skirt. She's a beaut!"

"Catch yourself on, Tod," said Bobby. "That's Jackie Brennan, sister of Seán Brennan who got out about a year ago. She's married, so forget about it."

"Oh look, Raymond. There's Mrs. . . . what's-her-name . . . Massey, your wife, looking at us," said Bobby.

"Don't let her hear you call her that. She's still Róisín Reynolds," said Raymond.

Róisín and Pauline, Bobby's girl, approached the men.

"Where's Sal?" asked Tod. Their baby, Nuala, was being minded by Tod's mother.

"Here she comes now, with Chrissie," said Raymond.

The children were being herded in and Chrissie was encouraging them to dance. Some did, some with natural grace, some showing off, whilst their mothers and fathers sat laughing and comparing.

"Right, you!" said Pauline to Bobby. "It's time you asked me for a dance. And you, Massey. The bride's waiting."

"I don't have to dance, Bobby, do I?"

"'Fraid so, groom. It's traditional."

"Then we get stuck into the bride's family, 'your da's nothing but a wanker,' etc.," said Tod.

"Tod, shut up," said Bobby.

"But I can't dance," said Raymond.

"Shut your face and go get Róisín," said Pauline.

"Okay, but I'll plug the first one who laughs."

"Jesus Christ, will you look at the way he walks," shouted Tod aloud, as Raymond went over to Róisín's table. Raymond stopped, turned, and waved his finger at Tod, whilst everyone enjoyed his discomfort.

The band was playing "Wonderful Tonight" as they took the floor, Raymond and Róisín first, Pauline and Bobby next. The newlyweds danced slowly and when Róisín kissed Raymond the room erupted in clapping and cheering. Pauline and Bobby, who had been necking, looked up and Bobby's and Raymond's eyes met. A dark cell covered in their own excrement, wriggling maggots emerging from their hive of rotting food in a corner, screams from somebody being beaten echoing along the landing . . . wondering would it ever end, would they get out alive. And here they were. Drunk and dancing, carefree. Bobby winked and Raymond smiled.

When they next looked around, the floor was filling up. Róisín's mother and father looked splendid and funny, Mr. Reynolds dancing as if he were participating in a ballroom competition. Gerry had his lips glued to Chrissie's mouth and the two of them hardly moved from the one spot. And even Aidan, in his dickie-bow, waistcoat and dress trousers, danced opposite one of his cousins, Lilian's daughter, both of them moving with an innate gracefulness to one side, lifting a foot, moving back and across to the other side and lifting another foot. Mrs. Massey talked non-stop to Jack as they circled, then was delighted when Mr. Reynolds asked her to dance.

He admired her earrings.

"They were my mother's," she said, and told him how she'd lost them, then found them after the prompting of a fortune teller the year before.

"You really should go and see her," said Mrs. Massey. "She's wonderful."

He smiled.

"I'm glad to see our Raymond married. I hope he'll settle down and take good care of Róisín."

"I certainly hope so," said Mr. Reynolds.

After several more dances the friends drifted back to a table. Chrissie and Gerry had joined her mother and Jack. Raymond was feeling elated. Tod and Sal were avidly listening to Raymond and Bobby reminiscing about their prison experiences.

"Why is it always like this?" said Pauline. "I thought they hated jail," she laughed.

"Listen out for 'the Winter of '78'," joked Róisín.

When Bobby and Raymond – schoolfriends – joined the IRA they had both just turned seventeen. Bobby made Raymond promise: "If I get killed and you're still around when the Brits are pulling out, I want you to come to my grave and shout into it, 'We've won, Bobby! We've won!' And I'll do the same for you."

Raymond had thought it a bit melodramatic and sentimental but shook on it and gave his word. He couldn't give a damn about his own body: when you're dead, you're dead. Beyond hearing. Beyond knowing.

"Raymie used to entertain us at nighttime," said Bobby, "by singing out the door."

"And now he sings to me at nighttime," said Róisín, curling her fingers around his.

"So what did you sing?" asked Pauline.

"What did he sing? He sang songs of defiance," declared Bobby quite proudly. "And sad songs. He sang sad songs."

"God, not 'Four Green Fields'," said Pauline.

"No, not that," said Bobby. "Songs about Joe Hill . . ."

"About who?" said Róisín.

"Nobody," said Raymond, reeling in the conversation.

"He was also good at 'The Croppy Boy.' Weren't you, kid?" said Bobby.

"The Croppy Boy," reflected Raymond. A sad rebel song. A *sentimental* rebel song! He smiled at the thought of this harmless contradiction, then remembered that he had sung to maintain morale, to fire the men with resistance. That's why he'd sung.

"Go on, give us a verse," coaxed Tod, but Raymond had no intention of singing. "What about you, Bobby?" said Tod. "You give us a song."

Bobby was drunk and began singing:

> As I was walking down Thomas Street
> my own cousin there I chanced to meet.
> My own cousin did me betray
> and for one gold guinea swore my life away . . .

Bobby was back in jail, a cold winter's night, up against the door, hearing Raymond's voice and quietly singing with him.

"What's this! A wake!" laughed Raymond. "Quinn! Knock it on the head!" And Bobby obeyed.

"I wish you'd grow your beard again," said Róisín. "You look so sexy with it."

"It's too itchy," he lied. With the beard he was too conspicuous. It would have made him more easily identifiable during certain operations on which he couldn't wear a mask.

"It's time you two made your grand exit," said Tod. "The train for Dublin leaves in half an hour." Then he announced to the reception that the couple were now leaving. Raymond had gone quiet. Mr. and Mrs. Reynolds, Róisín's sisters, Teresa, Lilian and Collette, Raymond's mother, Jack and Chrissie, gathered around their table.

"Róisín, I'm sorry to disappoint you, but we can't go to Dublin."

She looked at him, the beginnings of a tiny sickness in the pit of her stomach. "What do you mean?" she asked, dismayed.

"We can't go to Dublin because . . . we're going to Paris!"

"What?"

The company knew about the surprise and had been on edge in case someone unwittingly revealed the secret.

Raymond produced the tickets. Róisín didn't know what to say.

"But . . . but my passport, I don't know where it is . . ."

He pulled it out of his pocket. She burst into tears and a cheer went up. Sal cried with her.

"Awww," said Raymond, putting his arms around her. "Come on, love. We've a plane to catch, champagne to down, frogs' legs to eat."

"Ugh! *We'll* not be going to France on our honeymoon," said Bobby to Pauline.

"Oh yeah. Who says we're going anywhere!" she replied.

"If you don't say 'yes', I'll sing again," said Bobby.

"Yippee!" shouted Tod. "The guys are falling like ninepins!"

"And so will you," said Pauline, coming to Bobby's aid. "Wait till Sal gets her mits on you."

"She already has. Haven't you, love?"

Sal smiled. It was one of the best days of her life, next to the day that Nuala was born. She felt so good in her new outfit, an expensive suit that Tod had bought her. She looked at him smiling, engaging with everyone. He was wonderful, she thought. He worked so hard, taxiing until two and three in the morning.

5

DOWN BY THE SEINE it was cooler. Róisín was lying down, getting the sun, dozing intermittently after their picnic of wine, bread and cheeses. She was having a great time, had seen all the sights. Raymond was reading the *Irish Times* which he bought at a kiosk in Les Halles most afternoons. He finished the paper before filling in a few postcards for friends in jail. Then he plucked a bit of grass and, mimicking the lightness of a stray insect, entangled it in the wisps of his wife's hair. She was fooled the first time, brushing it away without opening her eyes, but the second time she caught the stem of grass, pulled it from his hand, rolled over and tried to poke it up his nose. He was laughing so much that he couldn't defend himself properly. He shouted that the wine was being spilled and only then did she stop.

Children nearby who were throwing a ball between them momentarily stopped and looked, thinking the adults were fighting.

"I wonder how Aidan's getting on," said Róisín, propped up on her elbows.

"Do you want to phone him?"

"No, sure we'll be seeing him on Sunday."

"We'll have to get him something," said Raymond.

"I know. But what?"

"I'll think of something."

He was looking across the river. He took a sip of wine. She leaned on one elbow and let free-thought take scrutiny. His face was lined – a bit grim. His hair had a bit of silver in it. Attractive. Not overtly sexual. Gentlemanly. Gallant. Yet a stoniness. She had never seen him scan another woman, the way she'd noticed Micky do. She really liked that about him. Trust itself was a source of pleasure.

"Hey Mister, what do you do for a living?" she joked in a mock-Parisian accent.

"Pursue my objectives."

She should have foreseen such an answer and was slightly annoyed at herself for erecting a platform. Although, to do him justice, he had accepted her for what she was.

"Raymond, love, when do you think the trouble in Ireland is going to be over for good?"

"Oh, not for a long, long time. First, we've to sap the will of the British government, then we have to force them to tell the unionists that the party's over."

"But that could take for ever . . . Is it even worth it?"

"Of course it is. You want Aidan to be able to get a job without someone discriminating against him. You want him to be able to go where he pleases without being in fear of his life, don't you? I want a settlement. I want the prisoners back home with their families. I want peace, more than anybody. I want a normal life, to be able to take you on holidays like this every year and not once in a blue moon. It's the British who are the problem. They've no right to be in Ireland."

"I know. But they are. There's no getting away from that fact and from the fact that we have to live with it. Where's the compromise, Raymond?"

"That'll come at the negotiating table."

"I meant, with us? Aidan and me?"

"Oh don't be worrying, it'll not go on forever. I'm not sure if the British can take much more. But even if it takes just a few more years, what about *us*?" He turned and faced her. "Don't let the Brits ever come between us," he said. "It's the type of thing they rely upon to weaken people. Most people just wanting the ordinary things in life, a bit of peace, a bit of work, not challenging the injustices, anything for a quiet life. If I were one of those people you'd be bored with me in a week!"

She thought he might be right. Was her relationship with Micky as glorious and good as she'd once made out? For the thousandth time she considered the matter. Micky had been good in bed. Very good. Better than Raymond. As before, when she allowed that contrast to surface she felt she was betraying Raymond. She turned and kissed him, unwittingly reinforcing his complacence.

"Would you not prefer to try for a child sooner rather than later? Before you go to university, while we're still fresh and full of energy, before Aidan gets too old and uninterested in a brother or sister? You said you wouldn't have a child if we weren't married. We're married now." His eyes had a promise of wildness in them which she found appealing.

"I'll stop taking the pill, will I?" She sounded very positive.

"Are you sure?"

"Yes, I'm sure. Why not!" She smiled and she felt good.

"That's brilliant! Let's get back to the hotel!"

"I don't think it works that quick!"

Two days later Róisín said, "Raymond, I'm going back on the pill. I hadn't really thought it out. I'm sorry."

"You've nothing to be sorry about. I understand. It's your choice."

They returned to Belfast to their new house. It had been allocated just a week before the wedding. He still hadn't completed redecorating when he went back to active service.

It was a sweltering August afternoon and Raymond and Pat

Doyle were soaked in sweat. They had just unloaded explosives from a lorry. It was then driven away. The bags of explosives were stacked against the walls of a carpet warehouse, in its storeroom. They were to be made up into a bomb for an attack on an army barracks in south Belfast.

Ten minutes later Bobby and Tod drove into the yard in a hijacked van. Behind them they noticed a car which sped away just too quickly. Instinctively, they turned their vehicle and drove back out on to the main road but from all around jeeps closed in on them and armed men in plain clothes emerged from cars. Soldiers dragged them from the van and began beating them. Raymond had seen the van do a U-turn and realized that something was wrong. He heard the revving engines of the jeeps as they swept into the yard and shouted the alarm to Pat. Pat smashed a window at the back and scrambled through. Raymond pulled off his gloves as he ran to the back of the storeroom to follow Pat. He was just squeezing through the window when the soldiers and police came bursting through the entrance. The first soldier saw the disappearing figure and fired a shot.

Raymond fell from the window in a long drop to the narrow bank of a stream. He saw Pat go off in one direction. He decided his own course and ran in zig-zags across a field. He pulled off the overalls and he hid his pistol in a hedge, then turned and saw a helicopter surf over the roof of the warehouse and rise in the sky like a monstrous rollercoaster. It roared and shrapnelled the air into a million pieces. Raymond didn't think he'd been spotted. He hurried through a residential estate, then ran across the main road to a shopping center. The helicopter continued to rise so that its purview was now extensive. Raymond entered a café and ordered a coffee. He had just sat down and stirred the cup when the police came in and marched around the tables, asking customers for their names and proof of identity. One officer saw Raymond and smiled.

"Well, well, well. Who have we here, but Mister Massey.

And guess what. He's under arrest!"

Pat Doyle had escaped. He went across the border to lie low.

Tod was brought into the magistrate's court first, answered his name and was remanded in custody. He was so flustered that he failed to look down at the public. His solicitor protested that there was no evidence against his client and that he would be applying to the High Court for bail. Next came Bobby, his head bearing fourteen stitches and covered in a bandage, who faced the same procedure. Then Raymond.

He looked down at the benches and immediately picked out Róisín and suddenly felt a wave of sympathy for her. The prosecutor asked that he be remanded in custody. His solicitor opposed the application and said there wasn't even a *prima facie* case against his client, who was arrested in a café and was being linked without a shred of evidence to an explosives find a half mile away. He said that Mr. Massey had agreed to go on an identity parade and that as far as they both were aware he had not been picked out by the soldier who had opened fire on the bombers.

Raymond waved to Róisín, Chrissie and his mother. Then, among the blur of faces, he noticed Patricia, Bobby's mother and father, Sal and Mrs. Malone, who all waved back. Raymond turned to Róisín again. As he was being taken away he winked at her and saw that she was crying. Handcuffed, he raised two clenched fists to show the police his defiance. They smiled, gave him the cynical thumbs-up, considered him pathetic.

All three were subsequently refused bail, the prosecution claiming that they were part of an IRA unit suspected of carrying out numerous bombings. Detectives believed that it was led by Raymond Massey.

The three prisoners and their relatives were all in the same smoky and noisy room, along with other visitors and prisoners. Sal came in first and ran crying to Tod.

His mother followed behind. "Well, what sort of a mess is this you've got yourself into," she said.

"For God's sake, Mom, give us a rest. Are those the first words you could say?"

"Okay, your dad wants nothing to do with you. Is that better?"

"Did they hurt you, Thomas?" asked Sal.

"Hurt me? They tried to break my arms and legs."

Mrs. Malone softened. "By the way, your dad only said that. He couldn't get up today but says to send him out a pass. And I've left in money from him."

"Thanks, Mom," said Tod. "How's Nuala, Sal?"

"She's sleeping at nights now. She's wonderful."

"She's a little angel," said Mrs. Malone.

Ten minutes before the end Tod's mother rose. "I'll leave you two alone for a bit."

"Thanks, Mrs. Malone," said Sal. "How's your chest," she said. "Do they give you your inhaler?"

"I've got it in the cell but they wouldn't give it to me in Castlereagh when they were trying to force me to make a statement. But I made no statement, Sal, not one word!" She looked so proud of him. He looked at her and had a swell of affection. "Poor Sal. Don't you be worrying, okay?"

She smiled back, that lovely feature of hers: innocence, pure innocence, he thought. No badness, no malice. She smiled so much that a big tear grew in one eye.

"I was so afraid, but now I feel okay."

"I'll be out of here in no time, Sal. Just you wait and see."

"How serious is it, Raymond? Really," asked Róisín.

"The charges will be dropped. If worse comes to worse and it goes to trial we'll beat it. Believe me. It's a set-up. A set-up."

"That's exactly what I told my mammy. You had been decorating the house all week and had only nipped out to get paint."

He wasn't sure if she was saying that in case the table or walls were bugged or she really believed it or just wanted to believe it. He often played down his own role and was continually amazed at her naivety, at how she accepted his explanations which he sometimes gave glibly, hoping she'd guess that he'd been more centrally involved than she assumed, though he'd never have admitted to a killing. He knew his imprisonment would be a test of her resilience. She remarked that she was not going to let it get her down and that she still intended returning to college in the term just beginning to do more O-levels.

"Did the Brits do much damage?"

"They drilled through the chimney breast and ripped the kitchen cupboards off the wall. And they pulled the wallpaper off Aidan's bedroom, the stuff you'd only put up."

"Was he okay?"

"You know Aidan. Brave face but shaking underneath. He says he's going to paper it, just the way you did."

Raymond laughed.

After the visits the three men compared the reactions of their women.

"Pauline called me everything," said Bobby. "But she was one hundred per cent at the finish-up."

"Sal was a hundred as well . . . Do you think we're going to beat this, Raymie?"

"Of course we are!"

"Do you really think so? What about the hijacked van? The owner's statement? Your fingerprints?"

"Means nothing. Absolutely nothing. We'll be walking out of here before you know it," said Raymond. "And you have to buy me a pint, okay?"

"Good man, Raymie! That's what I like about you," said Tod. "Totally confident, always in control."

"Tod," said Bobby. "Sorry, but he told me the same thing the last time we were caught together, that we would be getting out."

"Well, we did, didn't we," smiled Raymond.

"Yeah, after seven years," said Bobby.

"That's me depressed again," said Tod.

"Don't be listening to Bobby. I haven't been wrong yet. Just wait and see."

Raymond smiled when he opened his first food parcel. Róisín had sent him a copy of *Cousin Bette*. In all his parcels was the full quota of biscuits and fruit, newspapers and books. She spoilt him. He felt guilty and on their next visit told her to cut back. Then he asked her how she was keeping.

"I missed my period and thought I was pregnant there," she said. "But it was probably all the worry and anxiety."

"How do you know you're not pregnant?" he said excitedly, not having listened in full.

"Because my period started yesterday, okay?" she said.

"Wow. Okay. Okay." he smiled, gesticulating and backing off, and she smiled as well.

She wrote him interesting, substantial letters, covered her day, quoted from articles that she had been reading. At times when something sparked off a memory she would refer to her childhood at length so that the picture he had of her was being continually refreshed. A rereading always revealed something he'd missed first time around. He was glad he'd overcome his doubts about marriage. He was confident that Róisín would survive the present strain. She had passed her first two O-Levels and being back at college would provide her with a distraction, he thought.

Chrissie and his mother came up on their own one day and his sister told him that Róisín never went out at nights, was getting it hard, particularly in the run-up to Christmas. He asked his mother to help out financially. She said she was doing her best, could her own family not help more? Raymond was secretly angry at the remark but repeated the question to Róisín a few days later.

Róisín blew up. "My family?! If it weren't for my family I couldn't live. My daddy gave me £100 towards presents. I'm telling you now Raymond, see, if you beat these charges I don't want you going near the IRA. Do you hear me?"

He didn't like being cornered.

"You know I can't make a promise like that under these circumstances. I could say it just to please you . . ." (*"I could say it just to please you . . ."* She hated those familiar words of his. They always preceded some declaration of useless honesty.) " . . . and not mean it."

She studied him bitterly. Oh yes, he had given her everything. Everything he could, bar his republicanism. You can have everything in this Garden but the fruit of this tree. But worse, their life together hadn't been a Garden of Eden but a daily struggle to keep heads above water, Raymond producing money only at the very last moment.

"Well, I'm telling you, Raymond. Enough's enough. You *were* doing that bomb and there's me telling my mom about you being set up. If I had been pregnant after our honeymoon you weren't going to be around to help me, were you? I'm telling you, I'm totally depressed."

"Listen, Róisín. I respected your wishes when you decided you weren't ready for a baby. Isn't that so? Did I complain? Did I accuse you of welching? No. I didn't. All I ask is for you to respect my views."

"It's the fucking cost of them, Raymond."

"The fucking cost? I've got off lightly and so have you in comparison to many people in this country. Now do me a big favour, will you?"

She didn't know whether to fight him. She was furious. She was afraid. She had seen him become grave and terrifying, but only with men, friends and comrades, out in the hall or in the kitchen. She knew he had an iron will but she had prided herself that he was on her leash. He had never lost his temper with her.

"I said, will you do me a favour?"

"What's that?"

"Go out. Go out to the pictures or go out to the pub with

the girls. It'll do you good. You're sitting around the house, constantly worrying. I never let the odds get me down, otherwise I'd be paralysed. We'll look back upon these hard times and laugh. Wait and see. Now, do as I say and go out. Socialize."

"I don't want to. The only one I want to go out with is you."

"I really appreciate that."

"Oh, I hate you," she laughed. "And I love you, you bastard."

"You need to go out; otherwise you'll become a couch potato."

"I can't afford to go out."

"Well, stop sending me up so many biscuits and chocolates and books and magazines. Use that money on yourself."

"I don't really have the time, between Aidan, looking after the house, doing my assignments."

"Well, I'm not one of those hypocrites," he said, "like some of the boys in here, who were chasing when they were out and who are now born-again husbands. I trust you absolutely."

"And so you should," she said. "Now give me a kiss."

After Christmas the forensic report came through. Raymond and his solicitor were able to discuss his defense now that the case was taking shape.

"The evidence against you is circumstantial," said the solicitor. "Fibres from your sweater were found on the overalls, and your fingerprints were on the window sash. Our forensic man will probably be able to show that the fibres could have come from a variety of sweaters. Now, what about the fingerprints. How do you explain them?"

"I know the owner of the warehouse, Jim Carson," said Raymond, confidently, having already done the homework on his alibi and those of Bobby and Tod. "Jim asked me to fix the window after it had been broken by vandals. He's prepared to make an affidavit and go to court if it comes to it."

"Well, let's get that done and have it ready, just in case."

6

"MY MATE SAYS would you like to get up?"

"No thanks," smiled Róisín. "I've a wooden leg."

"Who's your mate, anyway," asked Chrissie, out of curiosity. "Which one?"

"Davy!" he shouted across the floor. "She says, 'Yes.' She'd love to!"

"I did not," said Róisín, adamantly. "Tell him no."

"She says she's not gonna wait all night!"

Davy waved his hand, realizing that he was the butt of a take-on. His mate laughed and returned to him at the bar.

"He's only a child," said Róisín. "Look at the bum fluff on his lip."

Sal and Chrissie smiled. "Another drink?" asked Chrissie.

"No, this is my round but I want to slow down. This is my first drink in months. I want to be conscious to welcome in the New Year," said Róisín.

"What about you, Sal? Another shandy?"

"Yes, please," she said.

"I'll only take one if I'm paying," said Róisín, firmly.

"Okay, then. If you insist," said Chrissie.

She gave her sister-in-law the money and Chrissie went up

to insinuate herself into the throng of small queues.

Róisín was enjoying the music. A lovesong was playing. She would have loved to dance. Looking at the couples moving slowly on the floor, some kissing, she realized that a lot of life had been passing her by whilst she was at home rearing Aidan, cooking and ironing, cleaning a house, rushing out to college for a few hours, visiting jail three days a week. Before he was arrested Raymond occasionally took her out, usually to a republican function to listen to rebel music. She couldn't remember the last time she'd been to a dance. She felt a bit guilty being here but her thoughts were interrupted by the appearance of Tina Owens, a friend of Chrissie. Her boyfriend, Joe, was a sentenced prisoner.

"How was your day?" asked Róisín.

"Fine. I was up seeing Joe."

"And how is he?"

"Same as usual. Never complains. How's Raymond? Any developments yet?"

"I'll not see him till Tuesday so I don't know. But there's a rumor that Tod and Bobby may be getting out in the New Year."

"Raymond'll be next. Wait and see," said Tina.

Róisín took to Tina who was garrulous and witty and kept them in laughter with bizarre stories concerning her shopping forays, her mad family, her visits to jail and what prisoners' wives and girlfriends really confided to each other. This was Róisín's second or third time out with her.

"You'll take a drink," said Tina to the company. "Joe signed me out a tenner and told me to welcome in the New Year."

"No, honestly," said Róisín.

"Ach, go on," said Chrissie. "Don't be a spoilsport."

"How long have you been going with Joe?" asked Róisín.

"Since I was fourteen," said Tina. "We broke up once, at my doing, and he was wrecked. That was before he went inside."

"Did you break up because of the IRA?"

"Hardly," said Tina. The way she said it Róisín suspected that she herself must be involved.

"How long has he been in jail?"

"Six years."

"And you've been *visiting* him for six years!"

"Yeah. But it doesn't seem like it."

"He must be something special," said Róisín.

"Are you kidding! He's the ugliest man in the jail but just does something for me. Makes me happy. Makes me laugh. Yes, he makes me laugh and he makes me feel important and comfortable. We're going to Tenerife in two years' time when he gets out. And we're going to have a ball!"

"Are you going to get married?"

"I hope so. That's the plan anyway. His parents live in England and his brothers here don't look after him. I'm all he's got," she said, proudly.

"I can't believe you've stood by him for six years."

"That's nothing. There's been women running to the jail for ten and eleven years."

"I know. I feel sorry for them. They need their heads examined."

"I think you'd do the same."

"Oh, I don't know about that."

"*Raymond Massey's* wife. Raymond's a great guy, Róisín. He's the best. Without people like him we'd be lost, I'm telling you."

"This is our anniversary," said Róisín.

"Your wedding?"

"No. This time nine years ago Raymond and I were up to no good, welcoming in the New Year." She laughed and for a second it occurred to her that he had been a better lover back then.

"I didn't realize you knew him that long."

"I didn't really think about it myself until you mentioned

you and Joe. What about Joe? Does he never get down or jealous of you going out?"

"Not now. He did at the start and I just laughed it off. Don't get me wrong. I don't go with anybody else. But everybody needs to go out."

Tina turned to Sal, who'd been engaging Chrissie. "And how are you?"

"Dead on, thanks. A bit of a sore back but I'll survive."

"What's the cause of that?"

"I'm trying to get the flat done up for Thomas coming home."

"That's great," said Tina, though she realized that Róisín was bound to be feeling a bit down.

Hours after Bobby and Tod were caught, the owner of their van had been arrested and questioned. He had been afraid to incriminate anyone but signed a police statement admitting that he had been hijacked but giving the wrong descriptions of the hijackers. Months later the IRA traced him to a town in County Tyrone and approached him. He was told to make a sworn statement to the effect that he knew Bobby and Tod, had lent them the van to shift some carpet, and was intimidated by the police into saying he was hijacked. He was happy enough to do that. He had been worried about his reputation in his nationalist home town.

There was no party to celebrate the release of Bobby and Tod, just a few quiet drinks with more family than friends in a lounge bar. Róisín and Chrissie called in to show their faces. Róisín left after one lemonade, afraid that her presence might constrain their enjoyment. Chrissie stayed for an hour but declined to go with the two couples for a pizza.

Róisín went home and cried. She had never felt more lonely. She was convinced that Raymond was going to be given a lengthy prison sentence. Aidan came down the stairs and pulled her a tissue from the box. He said he'd make her tea, even though he didn't know how. The phone rang. It was Bobby.

"How are you?"

She burst into tears again.

"He's getting out, Róisín. He's getting out. Everybody's sure of it. Will you listen!"

"Oh Bobby, he's away for ever, isn't he?"

"He's not. He'll be out in a week. They're just being bastards because of who he is, you'll see. They've nothing against him. Absolutely no evidence. Are you still crying? Listen. Pauline and I are coming straight over."

"No. No. I'm okay, now. Honestly. Go you on. Aidan's making me a cup of tea." She laughed aloud at the idea. "I'm being spoilt. I really am fine. And thanks for calling."

"Are you sure?"

"Yes, I'm sure. I'm sorry for putting a dampener on your night, earlier."

"No you didn't. We miss that crazy bastard as well, you know. Wait till you've done seven years with him, like me! Don't forget, I was engaged to him before you!"

"Thanks for calling, Bobby. It was very considerate of you."

"We'll have a big party within the next two weeks, wait and see."

"Okay then," she said. "I believe you."

Róisín was cursing. It was midday and still she wasn't dressed. She was on her knees, down underneath the sink which was full of dishwater. She was covered in dirt and grime, trying to unscrew the ring of the s-bend, below which she had placed a large bowl. Just as she pulled out the pipe someone rapped on the kitchen window, then tried the back door. It was unlocked.

Tod came in but she couldn't move as she was waiting to replace the bowl in case it overflowed. Her brow had little freckles of sweat. Her silk dressing gown was open a bit.

"What's the problem?" said Tod. From above he could see the flush below her throat, then the white of her breasts, whose swell began unusually high.

"The pipe," she said.

He bent down and found it difficult to avoid glancing up her thigh. Without thinking she tucked in her dressing gown.

"Here. Let me do that," he insisted.

"I have it drained," she said. "I can't get the ring back on."

She placed a towel on the floor to protect his jeans. He was always well groomed. He tightened it within seconds and got up.

"Not going to ask me why I'm here?"

"What's up?"

"He's getting out tomorrow."

"Who?"

"Who do you think? Raymond!"

"Tod, don't joke. Are you serious?"

"Róisín. Raymond Massey gets out of jail tomorrow morning at about eleven thirty. They're dropping the charges."

"Oh God. Oh my God! Thank you! Thank you!" She threw her arms around Tod and squeezed him. He kissed her on the cheek as innocently as he could but was caught and captured by the warmth she exuded and closed his eyes for a second.

She smelt good, as if the day-before's perfume had never left her or had freshly blossomed overnight. Raymond was one lucky man.

"I'm sorry," she said. "Look at me. Your collar's covered in tears."

"That's okay. Isn't it brilliant? Didn't I tell you he'd get out, didn't I?"

He explained the background. Róisín was full of excitement, her thoughts racing. She put on the kettle with shaking hands while he cleaned the sink. She liked Tod. He was still a kid in many ways. You could see it in the way he allowed the fact that he was an ex-prisoner to crop up in conversations, and in the

way he assumed himself to be an authority on parenting. He
was well-mannered, handsome and could be quite funny. That
explained Sal being head-over-heels in love with him. Sal was
quiet and ordinary and it reflected well on Tod that he should
be so devoted to her. For all the initial grumblings of his family about Sal and the pregnancy they had taken to her and spoilt
Nuala. Tod's father had even bought him a car to taxi in and
already Tod was planning to buy a newer model.

"God, look at me," said Róisín, tucking her hair behind her
ears after she handed him his tea. "I'm not even showered yet."

"Oh yeah, I noticed," he said, bantering.

"I can't wait until tomorrow. I can't wait."

Raymond was standing in the kitchen with his arms encircling
Róisín's midriff, slowly dancing as she tried to make sand-
wiches. Sal was helping her.

"Who taught you to dance?" Róisín asked. Turning to Sal,
she said, "He was never like this before."

"Maybe all men should go to jail for a while," said Sal,
proud of having made what seemed an important pro-
nouncement, then immediately felt it was stupid and hoped
they would quickly forget it.

"I'm reformable," said Raymond. "But I know. I know. I'm
an awful dancer."

"No, you're not. You're the best," Róisín said. Sal smiled
at them. They had always seemed to her the perfect couple.
Loud laughter, heard above the music, came from the living
room.

"Tina has some laugh!" said Raymond. "She's like a
hyena."

"She's great crack and has been very good to me and
Aidan," said Róisín. "And she's very dedicated to your lot."

"Is she still going with Joe what's-his-name?"

"Joe McMahon? Yes, still going strong. Visits him all the
time. He's out in about eighteen months' time."

Tina was on the floor with Tod, who was a remarkably good dancer. He was twisting right down on his hunkers but regardless of her effort she couldn't go as low as him. Pauline sat on Bobby's knee in a chair in the corner. Between occasional kisses they were enjoying the spectacle of Tina and Tod.

At about three in the morning the last of the guests had gone home and Raymond and Róisín climbed into bed. They had made love earlier that afternoon, within two hours of his release, but she was in the mood again.

"God, I'm exhausted," he said.

"I didn't think you'd be able to sleep, with the excitement and all . . ."

"What time's Aidan back from your ma's in the morning?"

"Not early enough, says you. I'll be expecting the works from you from dawn," she said, smiling.

"That's right. Make me feel inadequate! . . . Okay, that's it, off with the knickers . . . Jesus Christ, she's taking them off, I don't believe it!"

"I'm not looking for anything. It's just too warm. I'm used to being on my own."

He ran his hand between her legs and she turned to face him.

"Give's another one of those awful rubbers," he said.

"No. We'll not bother with that," she said. "It'll be all right."

"Are you sure?"

"Yes, I'm sure." Sal's constant natter about the baby had made Róisín just a little bit broody, though she felt the risk of her getting pregnant was slight.

Both of them were much more excited than earlier and enjoyed each other. Afterwards, Raymond lay on his back and looked up at the ceiling, which at the time of his arrest he had yet to paint, having finished only Aidan's room out of the whole house.

"See tomorrow. No, not tomorrow. On Thursday I'm going to paint this house from top to bottom."

"What's the sudden hurry, now?" she asked.

"In case I get lifted again," he joked.

"Just you dare. You'll be back living with your ma and taking her and Jack to bingo."

"God, I couldn't stand that."

"Shall I put the light out?" she asked.

"Okay, love. Night night."

"Night night."

"It's good to be home."

"It's good to have you back," she said. But a shadow of doubt crossed her mind.

7

TINA WORE HER NEW herringbone tweed jacket with matching top and skirt. She had spent an hour making up and when Bobby complimented her on her elegance she asked him not to forget the shoes, a brown pair, the right one of which she put forward for inspection.

"Notice these are not for running in," she stated.

"Trust me," he said.

They entered the manager's office in a petrol station, Tina exhibiting the gun in her waistband. Bobby told him they needed to use the back of the premises, it was an emergency. The manager protested that their people had used his place just a month before, that the garage had been raided by the army just that weekend, that the IRA had continued to hijack his customers' cars after promising not to.

They listened to him but he was compelled to cooperate. The two men crossed the hall to the garage shop. The girl on the till was a sympathizer and had been expecting them but in front of the manager Bobby sternly gave her orders to behave herself and act normally. The manager walked Bobby out to the back and around the pits as if he was a prospective buyer. The mechanics vaguely suspected that something was afoot.

All chose the safe side of ignorance and worked away at an engine, welded on a new exhaust, sanded down the Isopon filling on a damaged wing. Bobby brought the manager back to his office.

Wearing overalls covered in grease and oil, Bobby directed a goods lorry into the back yard, then the gates were shut.

Pat Doyle, the driver, quickly alighted. Pat and Bobby disappeared into the rear of the vehicle where they removed boards from the floor and with great effort hauled out heavy-duty bags containing ground fertilizer. They stacked these against the wall and covered them in tarpaulin.

The lorry was then driven away. Tina had stayed with the manager throughout. From his office she could scan the main road.

"Back in a second," shouted Bobby to the three men, who continued to work as if nothing were happening. He went to the manager's office, told him things were going according to plan, and made a telephone call. A few yards beyond the garage, and visible from the showroom, soldiers were establishing a checkpoint.

"You smoke too much," said Tina to the manager.

"Is it any bloody wonder?"

"Relax," said Bobby.

"Look, I've appointments which I can't cancel. This place doesn't run on its own."

"Just postpone. Run everything an hour or two behind schedule."

"I've an important customer due here any minute. I have to see him. Furthermore, it'll look very odd if she's sitting beside me at the desk with that gun sticking out of her skirt during negotiations. Somebody might even think she's my girlfriend."

Tina threw back her head and laughed. "I'll take shorthand," she said.

"She'll take shorthand," said Bobby. "You can see your customer. How long will he be?"

"Twenty minutes, maybe a little longer."

"That's okay."

The checkpoint remained in place for over forty minutes. Shortly after it was lifted a blue van turned into the side street. Tina ran through the premises to the back and shouted to Bobby, "They're here! They're here! I think that's them!"

"Okay. Go back to the front and stay there," he said. He watched carefully, recognized Raymond in the driving seat, Tod next to him, before opening the gates.

"Road's crawling," shouted Raymond as he jumped down and opened the back doors to allow another man out. "Tried to get here earlier but our *friends* were outside. Everything okay?"

"Yip." Turning to the other man, an IRA engineer, Bobby said, "I reckon there's the guts of fifteen, maybe eighteen hundred. There's three primers, about ten pound in each. Cortex is in the sack. Timer and dets are over there in the shoe box. I told them fellahs that we're just shifting gear . . . What's the town like?"

"Three checkpoints on the Falls," said Raymond. "One on the West Circular, two on the Grosvenor, one on Broadway and the Donny, another on Kennedy Way . . . Right, let's get her packed and we'll see what's what."

They helped the engineer shift three forty-pound drums from the back of the van into which he divided the fertilizer and inserted the primers. Using jacks the barrels were reloaded. The engineer climbed in and linked the drums with knotted Cordex.

"Phone!" shouted Tina from the foyer.

"That'll be for me," said Raymond. He returned before a minute had elapsed. "No sign of movement."

He noticed the three mechanics becoming more anxious and talking in whispers.

"Listen, lads," he said. "We'll be away as soon as we can. We're trying not to hold you back."

"Mister," said one, stepping forward. "There's no chance of that going off, is there? I'm shit-scared of those things."

"No, no chance. It's not wired-up to a power-pack, okay?"

"If you say so."

Outside, clouds crossed the sky, met an illusive obstacle somewhere in the east and banked in thick masses, darkening and chilling the evening, making September more like January.

Tod paced the floor. Bobby began a conversation with the mechanics about a car he once had. Raymond awaited the phone call that was to announce a clear run but it never came. Eventually, he called his squad together and announced that the operation was cancelled for the night.

"Get your car keys," said Tina to the manager. "I've fallen in love with you." They left together but returned twenty minutes later and she reported a particular road clear.

"We're pulling out, folks!" shouted Bobby. "As you know, nothing has happened, so go home and keep your mouths shut."

Tod commandeered the manager's BMW and scouted the van driven by Raymond to a lock-up garage in a residential area preserved for such emergencies. Then he returned the car.

Raymond made his way home on foot through one of those gloomy drizzles that wounds and drags day down. He stopped in a sheltered place, waited and watched. A petrol-blue stain was washed over and drawn to the surface in blinking luminous rings. The rain turned into a downpour and danced off smooth cobblestones where the old road showed through, the way it would dance off the ground in the floodlit prison yard late at night and evoke a confusion of melancholy, usually about dead comrades, their sacrifice and how more onerous that made his task.

As he stood, his mind again became susceptible to that emotion but slipped away from his grasp, unnoticed, into his feelings in the aftermath of a forgotten act. Television: the slow-voice homily of the minister, a snatch of a strange hymn, rain on stained-glass windows, three waterlogged graves, widows and children crying. The chemistry for regret had been on the verge of precipitation when the rifle volley over the coffins and the sanctimonious look on official faces, official grief, had separated the elements and returned him to his own conceit, and again returned him now through vague consciousness into a state of certainty.

He shook himself down and buttoned up his coat. He took to the rainswept streets with confidence restored. He refused to make do with it, yet something kept dragging him down. There was a sadness about the few cars on the road: their slow pace, funereal silence, muffled headlights. The simple truth was that most people were at home, by their firesides, with their families, and he was out here. Among the people there could be just a small attitude separating the sympathetic but uninvolved from the uninvolved and unsympathetic. He didn't mind the extra burden he inherited from the former but he resented the indifference of the latter even though he had long known that the catalyst for change was always the tiniest part of the whole.

He was two hours late for dinner. The rain attacked his flesh and depressed him. He was burdened by the impression that he had been bombing the town for ten years and might have to bomb it for another ten. His stomach groaned with hunger, his limbs felt as if they'd no marrow. He counted his money. It wasn't much but he stopped at an off-license and bought a cheap bottle of wine, a can of beer, a can of Coke and a packet of crisps.

He expected the protective drop bars which secured the front doors to be up but the door opened to his key. When he entered the living room Róisín didn't lift her eyes from her book. He hated these silences. Aidan came down the stairs, two at a time.

"Easy, easy, or you'll fall," said Raymond. He handed him the can of Coke and the crisps.

"Thanks, Raymond."

"Róisín, would you like a glass of wine, love," he said. She didn't reply. "Have you had your dinner?" he asked Aidan.

"Yep. Hours ago. What were you doing?"

"Working."

"Huh." Róisín's remark was barely audible above the rustle of the page being turned. Then she said, "Tell Ireland his dinner's burnt in the oven."

"I heard," said Raymond.

"Mammy, can I go over to Joey's?"

"No. You haven't got your homework finished and it's pouring down."

"But you said . . ."

"Never mind what I said. Get up the stairs and do your homework."

"But you said that I'd have to wait for Raymond to help me . . ."

"Didn't I just say, never mind what I said! And anyway that was three hours ago."

"Go get your homework," said Raymond. "I'll help you and then you can go out."

"No. He's not going out and that's it."

"Don't be punishing him just because I'm late."

"Call this late! This is early for you. Oh, get out and don't let me see you for an hour!" she shouted to the child, who grabbed his coat and rushed off gladly.

Raymond put out his dinner, lubricating the dry potatoes and peas with a large dollop of butter. He turned the sauce bottle upside down, seeking its dregs, wheedling out just enough to cover a bit of sausage. He opened the can of beer and was about to put it to his mouth when he remembered Róisín's manners and went back to the kitchen for a tumbler. There, he opened the wine, poured out a glass, and on his way back to the living room table set the wine on the hearth at her feet. She said nothing.

He ate perfunctorily, with his back to her. Half-way through dinner he heard her sip the wine and place the glass down. That's better, he thought, and began to enjoy what remained of his meal.

The following day, Tuesday, Tina was wearing black jeans and boots. It was just after lunchtime. Bobby and a local Volunteer secured a premises, a small scrapyard run by two brothers, the younger of whom was out doing a recovery and unlikely to return that day. There the van with the explosives was moved.

For seven hours they tried to find a breach in the ring of steel around the city center. As on the day before, the checkpoints were lifted temporarily – as if for a tease – before being replaced or shifted just a short distance. Out of frustration, Tina and Tod proposed alternative targets on the south side of town, but Raymond insisted that the bomb was going nowhere but the original target.

Once again the operation was abandoned. Raymond told the old scrap merchant that he'd have to remain under arrest overnight. It was decided that only one person was needed to secure the base and Tod said he'd stay. The local Volunteer kept watch from beyond for any undercover activity.

Wednesday was another dull, wet, dreary day, and the delays and accumulation of risks were making them all jittery. The scrapyard owner was ordered to phone his brother before he left home and send him on a false out-of-town errand. Raymond, Bobby, Tina and the engineer were quartered in a friendly house near the yard when they heard on the radio an RUC announcement that a major bombing was imminent and the public should be on the alert.

"Think they know something definite?" asked the engineer, a man called O'Neill who, along with his brother, specialized in explosives. "Or is it a bluff?"

"Well, there was a similar warning a fortnight ago and nobody was planning to bomb," said Raymond.

"It could be the van," said Bobby. It had been bought at an auction using false papers and they had been worried that it might subsequently have aroused suspicion.

"Then there's the garage. Somebody there might've said something."

"This bomb's now worth its weight in gold," declared Raymond. "It's worth twenty bombs. Getting it into town will be a major boot in the balls to the Brits . . . and the unionists will go crazy."

"That's my plans down the tubes," said Tina. "I thought tipping off the cops would enable me to get to the jail today," she joked.

Bobby told the old boy that he could have their van, gratis. The catch was that it had to remain berthed until they could remove their belongings from the back the following morning. "As if I've a choice," he said, resignedly. When the brother returned, furious because of his wasted day, he too was placed under arrest.

That night, as the cinemas were emptying of their few customers, Tod stood kissing Tina in a shop doorway as police on foot passed by.

"How many times do I have to tell you," she whispered. "Keep your tongue out of my mouth."

"But orders are we have to look besotted," he said, mimicking a whining voice as if he were being forced to do something distasteful. As he spoke, a snatch of light caught that handsome smile of his and she warned him with a glance, but without anger. He removed from a deep pocket in his underpants the timing device of small watch and battery to which the detonator was attached. Snogging, but behind her back actually working in the light of a shop display, he delicately adjusted the minute hand to allow for a fifty-minute delay. Tina removed from her underwear a sandwich-sized packet of explosives which was passed between them. He pressed the detonator into the explosives, carefully putting the completed bomb into

Tina's handbag. They walked a short distance across the square. There was a tailor's whose arched entrance was secured by an old-fashioned portcullis. Tod slipped the bomb underneath the gate and pushed it along the black and white tiles which bore on a fantail the inscription, "Established 1910".

They walked away, hand in hand, and phoned a warning to a newspaper. Half an hour later a white flash rent the sky above the city center and the explosion blew in several hundred windows.

On three occasions the following morning, Tod drove the glazier's van into the town. Each time it was stopped at a checkpoint and searched thoroughly. He tried the Shankill Road but the van was even more closely inspected coming from there.

"This isn't going to work," he said. "We could slip the bastard across to the shops on the Lisburn Road or flush the fucker down the toilet, just as long as we can get on with something else. This has me a fucking zombie."

"If I want your opinion I'll ask for it," said Raymond, looking at his watch. "This bomb is going into town in one hour."

"Fuck, are we an air force now?" risked Tod.

"Tod, fuck up, will you, or I'll strap those drums to *you* and fly you into town."

The sirens from jeeps, fire-brigades, ambulances and bomb-disposal personnel carriers wailed throughout the city center. Streets were being sealed off, shoppers and office workers fleeing in panic from an unlocated ubiquitous threat. Outside Government Buildings, just yards from the office block which received a bomb warning, a uniformed man swung his cream-colored vehicle around and brought it to a sudden halt. He almost fell on to the road, staggered and screamed hysterically that there was a bomb in his ambulance.

Raymond kept his hand firmly on the gun in his pocket, the

gun he'd held pressed to the ambulance driver's ribs before alighting from the van in the thick of the confusion, a short distance away. He was ready to swing around and kill the first person to tap him on the shoulder. Through the streets he rushed with the people fleeing like Pompeiians until he got outside the gated area. Then he walked calmly up to the car driven by Tod, the door courteously being opened to him.

The next day Tod was to pick up Raymond at two o'clock but as he approached a street corner he noticed the muzzle of a soldier's rifle appear at waist level a few feet in front of him. Instinctively, as if this had been the object of his outing, he made a diversion into Dempsey's butcher's and joined the small queue. He had been avoiding the advance scouts of a replacement regiment who were out patrolling with the outgoing battalions and familiarizing themselves with identifiable IRA faces, ex-prisoners and republican houses.

The soldier changed position and squatted at the corner entrance to the shop, maximizing his defense. Jack Dempsey, son of the owner, sharpened his knife along the etching of the steel, a honing which slowed stealthily into extended hisses.

"Ay! Watch you don't cut yourself, mate," grinned the squaddie, turning over chewing gum in his mouth. He put his eyes to the scope of his rifle and scanned the late September afternoon world of busy shoppers, passing black taxis and cars.

A young woman and a little girl negotiated their way around the soldier and into the shop's cool domain. The child was a fat little innocent with sunned calves and immaculate knees. The soldier blew the child a big bubble, imploded it so that it disappeared into a hole in his pursed lips, and the child giggled. Tod recognized the woman and nodded. She smiled back. The child became idly occupied in rubbing her sandal in the sawdust, making pleasing patterns, then her attention was side-tracked by a loose thread on her white sock which she bent down and plucked and which was neverending.

More soldiers appeared, ran into shop doorways across the street and awaited further orders. Skully, a local wino and ex-boxer, was staggering along the road. He approached the soldier in the hallway.

"Fuck the English and your English queen!" he screamed.

"I'm Welsh, Paddy. Couldn't give a fuck."

"Then fuck the Welsh and Harry Secombe," said Skully, who rocked back and forth like the pendulum of a metronome. It was slightly comical but such situations could turn in a second. One wrong word, like a loose sleeve caught in a lathe, could drag life into its crushing vortex. Irish manhood called into question, a blow thrown, a plastic bullet fired at close range and some civilian lies gasping with an eye missing or worse.

But the soldier suddenly stood up, blew a bubble at Skully, and dashed across the road to take up a new firing position. Tod relaxed.

He was next to be served and he invited the woman to go in front of him, as if he were merely holding the queue for a wife or mother. Moments later, when the area appeared to be clear, he left. He looked back and was disappointed that she didn't notice or acknowledge his departure. He got the borrowed car and picked up Raymond. They traveled to a house in Andersonstown where Raymond was to meet the brigade operations officer. Tod waited in another room but could hear voices being raised next door.

"We risked our lives, do you understand that!"

"Think you're the only one who puts bombs out?" said Seán Brennan.

"Well, we'll not be putting too many more out," threatened Raymond. "You're supposed to be representing us to the Northern Command. . ."

"Like everybody else, you'll do as you're told. It's a directive and you'll not be allowed to change it."

"An hour's too long! We've had proof after proof. Bomb disposal officers are running right in and defusing them because they know they've got twenty, twenty-five minutes to spare."

"You'll not be allowed to put forty minutes on a timer, and that's it. You get clearance for forty, somebody'll think it's okay to go to thirty. It's cutting things too close. They'll not be able to evacuate on time and civilians'll get killed or injured. We're not going back to those days."

"Then there's no point in putting out car bombs. My squad'll not be doing any more. As regards civilians, the cops don't give a damn, don't clear areas properly. It suits them. Politics."

"Yeah, but at the end of the day the bombs that explode are still the IRA's not the RUC's. Listen, it was bad luck that they defused the bomb. It was a good job."

"Any complaints about the ambulance?" said Raymond, softening.

"Of course there was. I was coming to that. An ambulance isn't to be used again. That's a directive . . . Look, I have to be in Ardoyne, like half an hour ago, and we haven't even talked about next week."

"Tod can drop you over, or do you have a lift?"

"I'll use Tod, if it's okay with you."

They discussed Raymond's plans, his financial and material needs for the following week, and made an arrangement to see each other a few days later.

"Before I go. Do you want a fella from Andytown – good operator, did Castlereagh and kept his mouth shut?"

"No. You know me," said Raymond. "I keep a tight ship. Only trust my own squad. We've had no problems so far so why fix it if it isn't broken."

"He's a good, young fella. Would increase your scope."

"No, thanks."

Tod was called back into the living room. He noticed the photograph on the mantelpiece as being that of the young woman he'd seen in the butcher's a few hours earlier. She had been a waitress at Raymond's wedding.

"This your sister's house?" he asked Seán.

"Yes," said Seán. "She's the boss, wears the trousers. Her husband Willie is a decent bloke too, a sales rep who works day and night so that he'll have a good pension in his old age to hand over to our Jackie."

"She was at your wedding, Raymond," said Tod. "A waitress."

"Don't remember," he said.

Raymond checked the mirror on the outside of the window, which gave him a clear view of his front door. The callers appeared to be an old man and woman. The door was rapped again. He shouted, "Who's there?"

"Michael Brown, here. You know me. I'm an uncle of Frank who's married to Lilian Reynolds."

Raymond recognized the elderly couple and unbarred the fortified door.

"Come on in, Michael," he said before shouting upstairs, "Róisín, it's the Browns. We're going out to the kitchen."

Róisín stopped what she was writing and wondered what Frank's aunt and uncle wanted. She looked again at the question in front of her. It perplexed her. She would have to ask a friend in college the next day if she could remember how they were supposed to answer it. She sighed, then rose from her desk in case they thought she was ill-mannered and came downstairs.

Raymond had offered them chairs in the kitchen, a room smaller, more private, than the living room. The time was after seven and they could see pots still cooking on the stove.

"You haven't had your dinner yet," said Mr. Brown. "I'm sorry. We'll come back tomorrow."

"No. Not at all," said Róisín. "He's cooking tonight and our wee lad's at the swimmers. Would you like a cup of tea?"

"No thanks, Róisín."

"So. What can I do for you?" asked Raymond.

"Where are you going, Róisín?" said Mr. Brown. "It's okay. Stay."

Róisín stayed.

"We wouldn't be bothering you except we're at the end of our tether and we need help quickly. We could have gone to Sinn Féin but we were told that you'd sort things out much quicker."

"Fire ahead," said Raymond.

Their story was that twelve months earlier they had leased out their fish-and-chip shop, which was getting too much for them. The shop was located at the front of their house and they lived at the back. Mrs. Brown's nephew, Tony, Lilian's brother-in-law, said he could look after it and the arrangement was agreed on a handshake. However, Tony had ruined the business and somehow managed to borrow from the bank on the strength of the property. They were still receiving demands for unpaid wholesalers' bills. After months of bickering Tony had agreed to square them all and had assured the Browns that he had paid a final notice from the electricity board. He had, but with a cheque which bounced. Late that afternoon, Friday, their supply had been disconnected and they were going to be without power all over the weekend, until Monday when they could appeal the decision.

Raymond listened. "First things first," he said. "I know somebody who'll put you back on tonight. . ."

The old woman looked a bit nervous, as if she were guilt-stricken at the thought of condoning something so irregular.

"Don't be worrying, Mrs. Brown," said Raymond. "It's done all the time. When the meter man comes out on Monday I'll explain to him that I did it. He'll be okay. You'll not get into any trouble. Now, about Tony. I'm not sure if I know which of Frank's brothers he is but I'll need an address. I can't see him tonight but I'll certainly make a point of seeing him tomorrow."

"He drinks in the Hunting Lodge every Friday night," said Mr. Brown.

"Well, perhaps I will see him tonight, after all," said Raymond. "Leave it to me. He'll pay back what he owes you."

Mrs. Brown now felt reassured and was glad she had come, despite initially trying to talk her husband out of this approach. She nodded to him. He took out an envelope which Róisín presumed contained some money. She could read the look on Raymond's face.

"Here's something for your trouble," said Mr. Brown, placing the envelope on the table.

"Take that back or I'll be offended," said Raymond, firmly. "That's not why we're doing this."

The old man hesitated. Róisín lifted the envelope. "We're only too glad to help you," she said.

They thanked them and left.

"What a bastard," said Róisín. "Lilian was telling me about Tony always flashing money, boasting that he had five girls working for him and that he was going to open a chain of shops. He tried to touch for me at our Lilian's wedding, when I was about fifteen. Imagine doing that on two old people, relatives too. Can you get the electric back on tonight?"

"Dermot McKee's an electrician. He's done it before for me. I'll phone him now, in case he's heading out for the night. Would you watch the spuds, please."

Róisín, polite most times, had occasionally shown her pique at the relentless procession of callers to the house: people looking for Raymond and the IRA to sort out this and that problem. She always made to absent herself but sometimes the visitors, especially women, would ask her to stay, perhaps because her presence made it easier to talk. There had been mothers whose sons had turned to crime to feed a drugs habit; a mother who wanted her husband shot after her daughter revealed that she was being interfered with; a young woman, accompanied by her mother, who alleged that the brother of an IRA man had attempted to rape her. There had also been a lot of dross: petty rows between neighbors over children or gardens or parking space or squalid feuds whose origins no one could remember.

Sometimes Róisín listened incredulously. Afterwards, Raymond and she would discuss the problems and once or twice she thought she might have saved someone from being falsely accused or misjudged. Raymond's patience amazed her. Often she felt like throwing many of these constituents out the door for wasting her and her husband's precious time. These are our supporters, he would say. These people have nowhere else to go. She both admired and despised that quality of Raymond which allowed him to absorb all these problems. She began to resent not just the IRA but her entire community, her insatiable, complaining community. But because she couldn't take her resentment out on a body so amorphous she would often make Raymond the object of her anger.

After he left she sat at her desk, placed her pen down, folded her arms, sat back and stared into space and wondered what her life would be like without him, without the worry, without the poverty. Two failed marriages? Wouldn't that be a public statement about her lack of judgement? But that itself could not be allowed to be an obstacle. The freedom of being an individual again, even as a single parent, and life without Raymond, were, one minute, airborne dreams, and, the next were punctured by little explosions of fondness and affection for him. When he wasn't acting as a republican he was the best person in the world. And even that was too harsh a judgement. Even as a republican she could accept him. It was how it possessed him was the problem.

He returned a few hours later.

"Well?" she said.

"The electricity's on."

"And what about Tony? Was he there?"

Raymond laughed. "He was there okay. I recognized him right away. I called him out to the toilet and he said, 'I know what you want to see me about, but I'm sorting it all out.'

Guess how much he had."

"I don't know. £20?"

"And a bit. £180. I took half of it to pay the electricity people for the reconnection and told him he'd better see the
Browns on Monday and begin sorting out the other bills."

"What did he say to that?"

"He said he'd do it, okay, that he had needed a good kick
up the ass, and did I want a drink."

"Did you take one?"

"Bloody sure I didn't. All I wanted to do was to get back
home to you."

8

AFTER HE FIXED the puncture on Aidan's bike, Raymond left the house. He had tried his best to take time off and relieve Róisín but it had worked out as only a day here and a day there and from her point of view was useless. Even this morning, Saturday, two days before her first exam, he had to go out, meet Tod and pick up a booby-trap bomb for an operation twelve miles from Belfast. He had only gone a short distance when he experienced an eerie feeling, like a dog aware of a ghost. Once again he believed he was being followed by the undercover whose surveillance in recent weeks had almost led to his squad being wiped out. Two weeks before, Bobby, Tod and he had been in a house assembling weapons for an ambush on two detectives. Tina had been on her way to meet them when she spotted a suspicious van move into a nearby cul de sac. She gained access to the first house with a phone and immediately rang Raymond. He decided they should disperse right away. They had just left the back of the house and taken to the gardens on the other side when the undercover sledge-hammered the front door and rushed in ready to kill, only to find two rifles and clips of ammunition on a blanket on the kitchen floor.

Raymond now listened hard. He could hear nothing but presumed that a helicopter somewhere high in a clearing in the cloudy sky was coordinating the movements of plain-clothes soldiers. He decided to change plans.

He continued down the street, turned on to the main road and called into his newsagents for the *Irish News*. A dozen scenarios were being revised in his head.

"Paul. Is there anybody out the back could let you away for two minutes?" he said to the shopkeeper.

"Yeah, my sister's there. You need something done?"

Raymond scanned the road outside. It was clear. "Would you get her, please." He then quickly wrote a small message. "Paul, after you see me get into a black hack, allow half a minute, then take this to Tina Owens. She'll be in her sister's but not for long. Okay?"

"Okay, Raymie. Anything wrong?"

"No, but it's important you get this to her."

"It'll be done."

"Keep it in your mouth."

"My mouth?"

"And if you're stopped, swallow it, okay?"

"Okay," he sighed.

"Have you ever killed anybody, Tod?"

He slapped the perfect roundness of her bare backside and laughed. "Why do you ask that?" The question flattered him but in general he was beginning to find Jackie a bit tiresome.

"I don't know. Just curious." She rolled on to her back. "Why did I ask that, let me see?" She thought for a bit. "Well, we were always taught it was a sin, weren't we. And of all the commandments it's the most serious."

"Oh yeah. How come it's Number Five in the Top Ten?"

"I don't know. Is it?"

"Count. Fourth, honor thy father and thy mother. Fifth, thou shalt not kill."

"And where's getting laid?" she smiled.

"It comes just after. Number Six. So, you see, my good lady, you're not far behind!"

"Yeah, but then there's that other one," she said, as if showing off her knowledge of the Bible. "That one about, 'thou shalt not cover thy neighbor's wife'."

"'Cover?' You mean, 'covet!' " He grabbed her breasts with his hands and squeezed them. Then he sat astride her and kissed her. "Christ, look at the time, Jackie. Your kid will be back from your ma's soon and I'm due at a meeting. I'll not have time for a shower." He climbed out of bed and began dressing.

She vaguely wondered why he always put on his socks first. "When will I see you again?"

"I'll phone," he said. He didn't sound very sure.

"Willie should be away next Thursday. Phone after seven, won't you."

"Okay. But if I don't it's because I'm up to here." He didn't like being pressed.

"Take care of yourself, Tod. You be careful."

"I will."

On his way downstairs he took out his asthma spray and inhaled three puffs. He had been embarrassed to use it in front of Jackie in case she thought he was a wimp. During the night when his chest became tight he had to wait anxiously until she went to the bathroom before using it. When he closed her back door behind him, the real world presented itself and he became anxious, with thoughts of Sal and Nuala, the bombing he had to carry out, and perhaps dying, having come from another woman's bed.

Raymond left the newspaper shop. He'd been there for about fifty seconds in all.

Good. Nothing unusual in that.

He maintained his habitual scrutiny of passing cars and strangers so as not to arouse suspicion among his adversaries. If he overacted, they'd know.

Black taxi. Cyclist. Milk float. Taxi. Taxi. Furniture van. Mazda. Nissan. Taxi. Bus. Toyota. Wedding car. Motorbike. Taxi. Black. Car. Silver. Red. Blue. Taxi. Taxi. Peugeot. Black. Black. Faces. Faces. Faces. Smiling. Grim. Worried. Smiling. Preoccupied. People laughing. Arguing. Laughing. Kids popping sweets. A scattering of lives. The weave and the weft.

Brilliant, he thought. They're fucking brilliant. Not one in sight.

He waved down a black taxi going into town. A half mile into the journey it was delayed by an army and police checkpoint on the Whiterock Road.

"Will you look at these tramps. I'm in a bloody hurry," said a middle-aged woman beside him.

Raymond could have confidently told her that there was no chance of them being stopped.

Tina's been given the message by now. She'll understand and she'll need at least half an hour.

They were waved through the roadblock. Good, thought Raymond. Excellent. Nearing his destination he knocked on the glass partition behind the driver who shouted, "Wait to we get through the lights."

Raymond climbed out, handed the driver the fare but the driver smiled at him and shooed his hand containing the money away.

"Go raibh maith agat," said Raymond.

"Fáilte romhat," said the driver.

The radio was in a house which had been raided a number of times without anything ever being caught. Today, time was of the essence but he would still be careful to protect these supporters. He had to appear engaged, purposeful. He had to gain time for his comrades without being seen to be stretching it. He felt he could elude the undercover, get to the house, get the radio and be back on the street before they construed the breach in surveillance as dangerous and were ordered out.

He walked past a greengrocer's, looking at the fruit in the window, stopped and walked back. He joined the small queue which had spilled on to the pavement. But as soon as it was inside the shop he excused himself, pushed through it, and nodded to the woman behind the counter who assumed he had business with her husband at the back of the store. Raymond went up to the elderly man who was measuring potatoes into bags from a dusty sack. He had huge dirty hands.

"Open the back door and leave it open," said Raymond.

"What to hell do you mean? What do you want?"

"Irish Republican Army. Open the door and keep it open. I'll be back in a minute."

"It leads to nowhere, just to the yard and the yard's sealed off."

"Never mind. Open it up and stay here."

He did what he was told.

Using the windowsill of the old coalhouse in the yard Raymond scaled the wall. He crouched and listened. He could hear the faint buzz of a helicopter and then its hacking the air, but it was in the sky beyond the other side of the roof and he hoped its view of the back was cut off. He jumped down into the entry, ran up the alley and knocked on the kitchen window of number fifteen.

A man in his stockinged feet was at the cooker boiling eggs. He looked up with surprise.

"Frank. I need the radio," said Raymond through the half-open window. "I need it quickly."

"The door's open," said Frank. "Come in, come in. She knows where it is. Come on in to I ask her."

Raymond's blood was on the swell. He needed to hurry. The woman produced the radio from somewhere and joked about him signing for it. He checked the power.

"That's great. Thanks!" He put it in the breast pocket of his jacket.

He ran back down the alley, climbed over the wall and jumped into the yard.

"That's me," he said to the bewildered grocer.

"What was all that about?"

"Nothing. Nothing at all. Could you give's an apple, they look great."

"Yeah, sure. Are you coming back?"

"No. You'll be glad to hear."

He took a bite from the green apple and left the shop. Crossing the road he saw a man in a zip-up jerkin at the side entrance to Dunville Park.

That's one. Now, where's the others? How many cars have they?

He walked along the road a bit to see if he could flush them out. Nothing. He waved down a taxi for Turf Lodge but the driver indicated Andersonstown Road. On the far side, a silver Volkswagen Golf passed in the opposite direction.

Woman driver, male passenger. Baby in the back strapped to a safety chair. He wondered. Had it passed him earlier, up the road? Silver. The color silver had a subliminal tag. When was it? His memory faltered, as if it feared assuming moral responsibility, and he detested its indecisiveness.

He hailed another taxi. The driver scrunched up his shoulders: sorry, full. A Peugeot drove past. The driver, a man with unkempt curly hair, stared straight ahead, unwavering. Raymond laughed into himself. I am an armed undercover soldier was written all over the motorist's face.

An empty taxi finally stopped. He climbed into the back, facing the traffic following behind. The taxi was fairly new and rich with the smell of leather, a smell that caught and distracted Raymond so that for just a second he was lost in some sort of other life. The taxi stopped for more passengers. Raymond told himself to concentrate. For the next ten minutes, as his taxi approached the top of the Whiterock Road, he could see nothing unusual from the window and felt more depressed than relieved.

They've realized we were on to them, he thought.

Emerging from the taxi at his journey's end he saw the same Peugeot drive into the car park at the block of shops. There were now two on board and Raymond's adrenalin shot up.

Tina and Pat were in the same block, on the first floor, just above the Peugeot. They were armed and masked, and had watched Raymond alight. They awaited his radio message to indicate who was undercover and where were their positions. Further down the street were Bobby with a rifle and Tod with a radio. Their getaway vehicle and driver were in the street behind.

Raymond had no idea of Tina's location. In his note he had just cited the general area but thought that his comrades were at the best vantage point, further down, below the church, perhaps in a house or a number of houses along his route. But what if she hadn't got his note? What if she had received it and the Brits had also been monitoring Tina's or Bobby's movements and were about to turn the tables on them?

Seconds after Raymond left the taxi, a Housing Executive van pulled up at the wall, alongside the shops. There were three men in the front cab. He thought it strange – at the weekends each van had only one worker on emergency call – but then recognized the middle passenger and realized they were locals. Raymond turned into the twisting alleys of back gardens with their tall wooden railings and overgrown hedges.

"Raymond! Raymond! Look out!"

His heart leaped and he jumped to the side as Aidan and a companion on bikes sped past him in a narrow gap, laughing.

"Fucking hell," said Raymond. Behind the boys, and gaining on Raymond, was a thickset man, the passenger from the Peugeot. He smiled, opened his jerkin and pulled a revolver from a shoulder holster.

The bastard's going to shoot me, realized Raymond. He sprinted around the corner of the L-shaped alley to rejoin the street again, pulling out his radio as he ran. There, a car was speeding towards him, to cut off his escape.

"The Peugeot! It's the fucking Peugeot!" Raymond screamed into his set as he stopped short and narrowly escaped being tossed over the bonnet. The car driver braked, intending to put his vehicle into reverse.

"Peugeot!" shouted Tod from the porch of the house to Bobby, who was lying below a hedge. "Get the fucking Peugeot!"

Bobby stood up, saw the car braking and opened fire with a long volley as it went past him. The driver then accelerated out of the fusillade, mounted the pavement in a crunching noise and went crashing down a steep embankment on to another street below.

The gunman behind Raymond held his pistol in the firing position and retreated backwards up the entry, speaking into a hidden microphone.

As Raymond picked himself up from the ground another car came speeding towards him from the bottom of the street.

"Silver Volkswagen!" he shouted across to Bobby. "The silver Volkswagen's one of them!"

Bobby leaned over the garden gate and took aim. He had a clear view of its approach. He saw a panicking couple with their child in the back, as if fleeing crossfire. He put his finger on the trigger and hesitated. Raymond was boiling with frustration.

"Shoot the fuckers! Shoot them!" he was screaming, but Bobby let them go.

Tina and Pat had heard Raymond's broadcast and the shooting but they were both pinned down by the suspicious Housing Executive van, until Tina shouted, "Fuck it, let's go!"

They ran down the stairs, across the car-park towards the van but the passengers were all lying on the floor of the cab like non-combatants. Tina took the precaution of raising her pistol towards the couple in the Volkswagen as it sped past the van before she noticed the child in the back. A helicopter had come in from the mountain and the noise of distant sirens could be heard. People were filling the streets in their hundreds, young people running everywhere with bricks and bottles. A crowd gathered around Tina and Pat, admiring their guns amidst loud talk.

"What happened down there?" Pat asked a youth.

"The 'RA opened fire on a car! There's an SAS man stuck in the entry with a crowd around him. He's got a fucking gun. Are youse gonna go down and shoot him!"

"Whereabouts? What entry?"

"Down there on the right. Do you want us to riot!"

A five or six-year-old boy tugged Tina's jeans. "Hey, are youse in the 'RA?"

"Jesus Christ, somebody take this child home," Tina said to the crowd.

"Here comes the Brits!" someone shouted.

"Here comes the Brits!"

Stones and bottle were thrown at the first jeeps to arrive. Behind them Pat and Tina heard the crowd first cheering but then jeering when plastic bullets were fired. From the entry came the sound of several shots.

"Let's get out of here," said Pat.

They ran down towards their safe house. Bobby and Tod retreated through the back gardens.

The shots in the entry had come from the undercover soldier. He had fired over the heads of the youths to keep them at bay in the few minutes before his comrades came to his rescue. Around the area the soldiers made arrests.

That night republican homes were raided and wrecked in reprisal.

Róisín had heard the shooting and had been sick with worry.

She had called Aidan in. He said he had seen Raymond. About two hours later, a woman called with a message to say that Raymond was safely out of the area but couldn't come home until the soldiers and police withdrew. One second she was worrying about him: the next she was furious with him, cursing him. She went into the kitchen for something, lifted the mug she'd bought him on their honeymoon and smashed it on the floor.

How can I study under these conditions, she cried. How can I do anything with my life.

Later, she took a pill to calm her nerves and help herself sleep but awoke groggily with Aidan shaking her.

"Mammy, mammy, the Brits are outside!"

"Open the feckin' door or we'll break it down! Open it now!" shouted a soldier.

She rose and put on her dressing gown.

"I'm coming, I'm coming! Take it easy!"

She unlocked the security gate on the stairs, went to the door and removed the drop bars. She had hardly turned the snib when the door was pushed open and struck her on the temple. They rushed in and she didn't even bother attempting to limit and monitor their movements.

A policeman said, "Who lives here?"

"Me, my child and my husband."

"Where is he?"

"I thought you would know. Don't you know everything."

"Get into the living room. You are both under house arrest while we carry out a search."

"Can I go to the kitchen?"

"No," said the policeman. Then, "Have you been drinking? You look drunk."

She ignored the comment but was smarting.

They left after an hour.

Róisín felt like giving up all her studying. She had tried to do her best but there were gaps in parts of her course and she felt sure she hadn't done enough revision.

By lunchtime on Sunday Raymond still hadn't returned home. He was awaiting the arrival of other members of his squad for an assessment.

Bobby came in first. His mother's and Patricia's had both been searched.

They heard the garden gate opening. Bobby stood up and looked out the bedroom window. "It's Tina," he said.

Tina spoke to the householders and was directed upstairs. "Hear about Tod?" she said.

"What about him?"

"He was arrested last night."

"Where?" said Raymond.

"They did his ma's but he thought they didn't have his new address. They raided the house and got him. He's in Castlereagh now."

"The stupid bastard. Well, that means all of us staying out of the house for the next week," said Raymond.

"You don't think Tod would turn supergrass?" said Tina. "He's been through Castlereagh before."

"I doubt it, but you never know what the cops can hit you with. We'll just be careful until he gets out and we know what's what," said Raymond. "Was your place hit, Tina?"

"No. What about you?"

"I don't know the damage yet. I'm sure Róisín's not speaking to me. Her exams start tomorrow and I promised to look after Aidan."

"I'll call round and see how she is," said Tina.

"No. Don't be doing that. No movement until Tod gets out."

"But what about the jail? I've a visit on Tuesday."

"You'll just have to wait. I'm sorry."

Pat arrived with a local Sunday newspaper. They told him about Tod.

"Says here," said Pat, "that a family had a narrow escape. A husband and wife and baby."

"Does it name them? Say where they are from? Are they interviewed?"

"No, nothing at all."

"Then that's an RUC story," said Raymond, "and we should get a statement issued challenging it. Will you see to that, Tina?"

She nodded.

"Well, I thought there was a child in the back," said Bobby.

"There was no child, Bobby, and I can't believe you let that car go," said Raymond.

"I thought it was a kid in the back," said Pat.

"So did I," said Tina, hating to contradict Raymond.

"It was Brits. I saw them with my own eyes, up here, then down the road, and then up here again. None of you should have let them go."

"I'm glad I did," said Bobby. "Just in case it was. I was shooting no kid."

In the back of the jeep Tod was kicked and punched. He was ordered to lie on the floor and refused. A soldier slapped him across the head and he felt his eardrum pop and a hot trickle of blood gather in the horn of his ear. In Castlereagh he was examined by a doctor who recommended that he be taken to hospital. He was taken there under armed guard but was returned to the interrogation center with a suspected perforated eardrum. Under questioning he remained tight-lipped but picked up from the line of questioning that there was no hard evidence against any of them.

The RUC weren't certain of who played what role, apart from Raymond's part in the lure, and conceded that it was a clever ploy. They failed to disguise their resentment of the fact that they weren't entirely acquainted with the details of the undercover operation.

As Tod lay in his cell, his ear throbbed. He thought about Sal and he thought about Jackie Brennan. He had been seeing her for about six weeks. Since Sal and he had set up home together he had been unfaithful to her on six or seven occasions, or was it eight? Sometimes he counted those escapades, for the thrill. Most were unpremeditated, drunken half-night stands. But going out with someone else was in a different league.

Sal, to his disappointment, had never really initiated lovemaking, or, if she did, it had an aspect of sufferance about it. One night, after he had got her to drink more than usual, he had tied her to the bed to add a bit of spice, passing it off as a joke. She made no complaint but her frightened face said it all and he was caught between being sorry for shocking her and resenting her lack of imagination. Then he was secretly angry with her for making him feel dirty when he had done no wrong.

Jackie had been a late fare in his car. She had phoned from a party. He waited outside the house, impatiently beeping his horn, and was ready to drive off when she came out and apologized for the delay. Once in her seat she declared, "I couldn't get my coat from the bedroom because somebody was getting laid." She was speaking in the risqué way that people sometimes do when their tongue is loosened by drink, though not necessarily their morals.

"Still wearing the wee black skirt?" said Tod.

"What wee black skirt?"

"Aren't you a waitress?"

"I was. But how did you know?"

"Spying on you." He wouldn't elaborate.

She reached for her bag and her hand brushed his thigh. "Sorry," she said.

"That's okay."

She put her hand back on his thigh and squeezed it. Tod got the hots for her. She kept her hand there for the remainder of the journey even though the talk turned to other subjects, and her grip tightened when he turned a corner or braked approaching lights. In her street she told him to pull up, short of her door.

"Fancy a drink sometime?" she asked.

"Sure. That would be great." He arranged to meet her four nights later in a hotel in the south of the city where few would know them. That day he had been full of beans, contemplating the exciting night ahead, wondering where later they could privately go. He had sat waiting for two hours and she didn't show up. He had given her the telephone number in case some problem had arisen but she didn't page him. He was angry with her but now wanted her all the more. When he next saw her she was out shopping with her daughter. He got out of his car, walked up behind her and tapped her on the shoulder.

"Hi!" she said, turning.

"Hi. What happened to you last week?"

"Last week? Oh, last week. I'm sorry about that. Were you there? I couldn't make it. Something cropped up at home. My husband took sick, didn't go away."

"You could've phoned."

"I forgot the number and couldn't find it."

"You missed a great night," he said.

"Oh well. Sorry about that." Her child was tugging at her sleeve. "Maybe some other time. I'll have to go before she pulls this sweater apart."

"See you," said Tod, disappointed, wandering back to the car.

Then, a few weeks later, he picked her up again, late one night.

"Another party?" he said, when she stepped into the car, bringing an air of pleasant perfume and the sweet grainy bouquet of vodka on her breath.

"A hen night. My friend's getting married."

"Couldn't you have talked her out of it?"

"It was me talked her into it," she said. When they arrived in her street, she said. "Is there not somewhere we could go?"

Tod leaned over, took her face in his hand, kissed her hard, then groped her firmly just to make sure he wasn't misunderstanding, and she moaned. Her breasts were much firmer than Sal's.

He took her up the mountain, found a deserted lane and in the car he and Jackie made love. Sal kissed like her lips were clamped and only lately had she begun making noises that sounded as if she was experiencing pleasure. Jackie, in her language and expressions, her excitement and daring, had been so uninhibited that for the following few days he thought that love of her body was love of her soul. But after a month or so he suspected that it was merely the novelty that had fooled his emotions. The orgy of new experiences began to take on a blandness whereas it now seemed that there was something else to love-making with Sal: his old relaxed confidence, perhaps love itself. He chewed over the fact that in Sal's company there was contentment. Sal knew more about his habits than he did himself. Lying in his prison cell he felt good when he decided that he was going to break it off with Jackie and give Sal and him a chance.

Tod was released after four days. Two days later he was debriefed by IRA security and satisfied them that he hadn't broken or entered into any deal.

9

RAYMOND CAME HOME after Tod's release, an afternoon when Róisín was out at college sitting the second part of her exams. He had telephoned her the night before, for the second time, and for the second time she'd hung up.

He entered the house and it seemed as if he'd been away for months. He put the drop bars on the front door and immediately felt more secure.

The smell of Róisín's perfume hung in the air. He went upstairs and saw her books scattered over the duvet cover and realized that she must have been studying up until the very last moment. In the basket underneath the dressing-table he saw an envelope torn in two. He couldn't understand why his name was on it. From within he pulled out two halves of an anniversary card and realized he had forgotten that they were two years married.

Making the bed he picked up her nightdress, held it up to his nostrils and inhaled deeply, as if he could discern from her light perspiration the contents of her troubled mind. He washed the breakfast dishes, cleaned and tidied up the house. He checked the cupboards and fridge and prepared dinner. When Aidan didn't come home from school he telephoned

Mrs. Reynolds, who said that he was staying with her, that Róisín was going out with Chrissie, Tina Owens and some friends from college for a meal and drink after her exam. He was annoyed at Tina for not mentioning this to him. He asked to speak to Aidan. Aidan said that he wanted to stay in his granny's, he was afraid that the soldiers might return and was that okay. Raymond said it was.

The evening stretched out before him. He watched the news programs on TV, read a book, got bored, walked around the room, made himself tea, couldn't settle. He began to worry. She was never this late. She could have been caught in a bombing in a restaurant, or a shooting if loyalists had recognized Tina. He switched on the one o'clock news but all that was reported were shots fired through someone's window and an incendiary scare in Bridge Street. The main item of the day was repeated: the RUC Chief Constable boasting that another "converted terrorist" was responsible for the recent arrests of thirteen suspects.

Ten minutes later he heard her key in the door and the door rattle against the drop bars. He rushed to the hall to let her in.

"Huh," she said, and walked in, kicking off her shoes. "I know you from somewhere, don't I?"

"Where were you, I was sick with worry!"

"Huh." She sat on the sofa and laughed. Awkwardly she arose, went out to the kitchen, opened the fridge door and tutted with disappointment. She returned and fell down into the sofa, laughing.

"I made you some dinner but then your ma told me you were away out for a meal."

She continued to laugh.

He didn't like the frock she wore; it was too low-cut. "What's so funny?"

"Tina and your Chrissie."

"What about them?"

"We were in this pub, right? After the others left."

"What pub? What others?"

"We were in this pub and Chrissie went up to the bar to get a drink. Just as she was leaving the barman leaned over and said, 'Excuse me, but is your name Massey?'

"'Yes,' she said. 'Why?'

"'Ach, years and years ago I went to school with your Raymond.'

"'What's your name,' said Chrissie, 'and I'll tell him I was talking to you.'

"Some name. He said some name and said you'd know who he was. He said you left school the same year . . . Then he said to Chrissie, 'Tell me this before you go. Whatever happened to your younger sister? Chrissie, I think her name was? I used to be crazy about her. She had lovely long hair.'

"'Are you serious?' said Chrissie.

"'Oh aye, I fancied her okay. Nice girl.'

"'I mean, are you pulling my leg?' said Chrissie.

"'What about?' he said. Chrissie just turned on her heels and was put in a really bad mood. Okay, her hair's shorter but I mean to say, she couldn't have changed that much."

"Did he say anything else? Did anything happen?" asked Raymond.

"Did anything happen! He came down to our table to see what the fuss was about and I threw a pint around him and then we got thrown out."

"You what! Where was this? Was it on the Road?"

"No, it wasn't on the frigging famous *Road*. It was downtown, in the Washington."

"What did you make a scene for? Where was Tina when all this was happening?"

"She glassed the bouncer."

"She what!"

"Then she pulled a gun on the crowd trying to get at us."

Raymond burst out laughing. "You bastard. You had me believing that."

"No chance of anything as exciting in my life. Not like yours," she said, cynically. "But the barman did say that to Chrissie."

"Well, how did your exam go?"

"I'd prefer if we didn't talk about it."

"I'm sorry about what happened."

"I'm sure you are but I don't really care any more."

"What about?"

"Anything. The life you lead, the way you come and go like a glorified lodger. The way you just manage to squeeze me in." She sat forward and bent down to check the red polish on her toenails: they looked as if they had been dipped in blood.

"I don't come in drunk, do I?" he said. "I don't gamble? I don't run to dances or discos. . ."

"More's the pity. You'd be a bit of fun."

"I take Aidan to the leisure center, do his homework. . ."

"Aidan! Why do you think that child wets the bed? Well?"

"I clean around the house, don't I," he said, ignoring her comment.

"The house! Look around this house. You don't even see it, do you?"

"See what? I cleaned it from top to bottom today."

"Not see anything wrong with it?"

"No. Have you moved the furniture around?"

"I despair."

"What are you going on about? I think you're drunk."

"First, the fucking RUC! Now you!" She jumped up, startling him. "Drunk, am I!" She lifted the ornaments in turn from the mantelpiece, then the clock and threw them crashing on the hearth and floor.

He was stunned at her sudden change in temperament. He had been given no warning. As suddenly as she had become enraged she became distraught and began crying. He stood up to embrace her but she pushed him off.

"Look around us, Raymond. Have a look at the way we

live," she sobbed. "We've no money and no prospects of money. The furniture is years old, bought by Micky. Remember him? You know, I'm even ashamed when the Brits raid this house, it is so rundown. You promised ages ago to fix the guttering. It's me has to listen to it dripping on the nights you aren't here." Tears were spilling down her cheeks and there were tiny bubbles between her teeth and at the sides of her mouth. "I'm paying off the kitchen cupboards and washing machine. You're on the dole. The movement gives you £20 a week. You said yourself that sentenced prisoners could do their time okay but that it was hardest on the lifers who didn't have a release date. So tell me, Raymond, I want to know. How long do we have to live this way? What's our release date?"

"I'll see if I can borrow some money from the 'RA, okay?"

"The 'RA, the 'RA, the fucking 'RA. I hate you and the fucking 'RA! Get a job like any honest person!"

"Keep your voice down, the neighbors'll hear."

"The neighbors! They all think you're such a gentleman but in fact you are one bastard. You love the IRA more than you love me and Aidan. What did you ever marry me for!" She wheezed and sobbed.

"Don't give me that nonsense, Róisín," he said, trying to instill some sense. "You knew what you were getting yourself into. . ."

"I didn't! I didn't!"

"You knew what I was doing, you knew I'd been in jail. I told you no lies and I made no false promises." He felt like confronting her with her contradictions: her appearances by his side at the wakes of Volunteers; her cursing the TV when Thatcher was on speaking about Ireland; her socialising with Tina, a Volunteer; with Chrissie, a sympathizer; with Sal, a Volunteer's wife; with Patricia, a Volunteer's girlfriend.

"Raymond, please. Please." He noticed her eyes were suddenly bloodshot. "I beg you. Give it up. It's going nowhere, you must know that. Look at that child shot dead last week.

A wee baby. What cause can justify that? It's shameful. When I heard that, my stomach turned. I thought, if we had a baby coming into a world like this. . ."

"Exactly! This world is stinking, it's wrong and somebody has to change it. It involves sacrifice, Róisín. You must understand that. You do understand that. I can't give up. That would be an act of surrender and defeat. What a victory for the Brits that would be! And what would that make of my past actions? A pastime? Now I'm bored so I'll try something else?

"The things I did I did on the principle of consistency to the end. I accepted jail and I accept death as the possible price of my actions but I'll never accept defeat. To stop now would make my past actions wrong, immoral. I am following my conscience."

"You're full of conceit, do you know that," she said quietly and confidently as she held a balled hanky in her hand.

For a few seconds her comment cut him to the quick. Were altruism and arrogance just two faces of the one coin? Was he elitist and self-righteous? He could feel a little wave of contempt rise within but remained calm. He knew he was right. Somewhere a house was being wrecked. A soldier sat on the end of a bed reading someone's personal love letters and an RUC man rummaged through drawers, pawing over a girl's underwear. A British cabinet minister drank brandy and nodded clearance for an assassination. At the end of a sumptuous meal in a big house across town guests were having a laugh and the promotion prospects of a Catholic colleague were being fed to the dogs along with the left-overs. Out there now, loyalist cut-throats were cruising the streets for a late-night victim. She must know that he could never change.

"Would you like a cup of tea?" he asked.

She was totally exhausted, had been sucked down into the crevices of the old sofa.

He thought maybe she hadn't heard. "Róisín, love, would you like a cup of tea?"

She looked up, then replied, "Yes, please." She looked at her wristwatch, then asked the right time.

"I'm not sure. The minute hand's pointing at the TV and the hour hand at the coal bucket."

She smiled. Smiled poignantly.

Half an hour before the prison officer was due to leave for night duty Raymond and Tod drove up outside his home. Raymond quickly alighted, boldly walked up the driveway, rolled under the car and attached the bomb to the chassis. From his pocket he took out a cellophane bag and from it coaxed a dog turd on to the tarmac, inches from the driver's door, to deter the prison officer from kneeling down to examine the underside of his car.

Within twenty minutes Raymond and Tod were back in West Belfast. They returned the borrowed Vauxhall to its owner and then headed to the pub where Raymond's car was parked. Tod's was two streets away. They took a table in a corner within earshot of the local news due shortly on the television and ordered soft drinks. By now the bomb should have exploded but the main item on the news was the conviction earlier that day of fifteen people for a series of offences on the word of a former comrade who had turned state's evidence.

"Bastard," said Tod.

"Never mind him. Our yoddler hasn't gone," said Raymond.

"Maybe he hasn't gone to work yet. Maybe the July schedules are all up in the air."

"He's been on duty all week. He had to be at the jail for eight o'clock. The intelligence was a hundred."

"Maybe his kid took sick or something."

"No. He has one son and daughter. One's in America and the other's on holiday in Greece."

"Well, maybe it's went and the news hasn't got it yet."

"After all that work. Get me another orange," said Raymond.

"What are you doing about grub? I'm not hungry myself but Sal'll make you something in no time."

"It's okay. I've to see our Chrissie about something. I'll be fine, thanks."

Tod was at the bar when soldiers entered, part of a regiment on its last week of duty. They stayed a short while, checked a few identities and then left. When Tod returned to the table Raymond was still fuming.

"I can't get over that bloody job not going."

"You should know by now. Win some. Lose some."

"I know, but when that bastard was an ordinary screw he used to beat the shite out of me and Bobby and the boys. We'll never get another chance like that one."

"Don't you just love it when the Brits pretend not to recognize you!"

"They're probably on the phone now to the loyalists," joked Raymond.

"That quickly?" said Tod, smiling.

They came out of the pub and carefully looked around the street for strangers. Tod told Raymond to go on, that he'd forgotten to make a phone call.

He had made up his mind, not for the first time, to break it off with Jackie. He phoned but her husband answered. Tod thought Willie would have been away on business. He put down the receiver, went for his car and headed to the depot where he reported for work. As he drove about he considered what to do. He decided not to call Jackie, then knew he was only postponing the inevitable. He stopped at a phone, dialed the number and she answered.

"Oh, hello. Was that you earlier?"

"Why? Did he say anything?"

She laughed. "He said it was probably a wrong number."

Her good mood irritated him, the ease with which she could

carry off deceit. She had once told Tod that even if her husband caught them in bed red-handed she could have convinced him that Tod was only mending the springs.

"He'll not be back until tomorrow night and I can get
Jacqueline in bed and fast asleep by ten. Get a Chinkers on
your way. I've drink in."

He allowed silence to speak for his difficulty, then said, "I
need to talk to you."

He knew she knew why but she dissembled.

"I need to talk to you as well. It's been ages. Don't worry if
you can't get here till late. I'm not a bit tired. And I've got a
surprise for you," she said in her coquettish way.

He sighed. Another silence developed, one in which she
knew Tod's lust was rumbling and she experienced something
just short of smugness. Yes, he was now in two minds.

"Okay. I'll see you around half twelve," he said, and
thought, what excuse will I make to Sal?

"I'll see you then, Tod."

"Bye."

"Bye, Tod."

"Bye-bye, Tod," said Jacqueline, Jackie's daughter. He
slammed down the diseased receiver. The wee bastard must
have been on the extension the whole time! he thought, wondering would she say anything to her father.

"Fuck that. Jackie'll not be seeing me tonight. She'll not be
seeing me again."

He told the depot manager he had to go off duty.

Sal would peck at food like a little sparrow but she liked
pizzas. Tod bought a pizza with an olive topping, her favorite.
When he arrived at the house Sal and Nuala had their coats
on.

"Where are you two going?" he asked, disappointed.

"I'm taking these empty bottles to the off-license to get you
some beer," she said, indicating the contents of two plastic

carrier bags. "I'll have to hurry, it's almost ten o'clock."

"Sal, Sal," he said. "We don't need to bring back empties. Throw them in the bin."

"But there's still only two beers in the fridge."

"That's okay. They'll do."

"Are you home for good?" she asked.

"Yes. Now, coats off. Get your bums on the sofa. Nuala, would you like some pizza?"

"Yes, daddy," she said, shaking her head vigorously.

He put plates in the oven to heat, then came into the living room.

"Open your mouth and close your eyes," he said to Nuala. She opened wide and he popped in an olive. Nuala's face screwed up into the face she made on the day she was born and she rolled out her tongue with the mashed olive dangling on its tip. Tod held out the palm of his hand.

"Go ahead. Spit it out," he said, and after she did, she looked first at her father, then her mother and back at her father.

"Ugghhh!" she said, in delayed response, exaggerating, and they both laughed.

Tod switched on the ten o'clock news. It was reported that police had sealed off a street in Bangor and that bomb disposal experts were examining a suspect device found by a prisoner officer underneath his vehicle.

"I called in to your house," said Tod. "Róisín said you were out on business all night and she didn't know when you'd be back. Is there anything wrong? You look shattered."

"No, everything's fine. I ended up in our Chrissie's at four this morning where there was a party still going on."

"Wish I'd known about that."

"No you don't. I drank more than I've ever drunk before. Fact, I'm still drunk. I think."

"Where were you to four?"

"What happened was that I got some *scéal* and went to have a look at a bungalow three Branchmen from England are supposed to be billeting in. I went back and forth but there was no sign of their cars. Must have been bum info. It would have been a beezer too. One driver, one guy to plant a charge. Anyway, no harm in trying."

"By the way, I've something for you," said Tod.

"What is it?" said Raymond as Tod handed him a shopping bag.

"Open it up."

Inside the bag were new clothes: a pair of jeans, a denim shirt and a light, summer jerkin; and new trainers.

"Who are these for?"

"They're for you. I got them for you yesterday. Weren't you going on about needing a shirt and things."

"Tod. I can't accept these."

"Don't offend me. I'm taxiing, I've more money than you, and, besides, they cost very little. My cousin's a manager in the shop I got them."

Raymond was embarrassed.

"Try on the jeans because I can get them changed."

"I hope Tina doesn't come in," said Raymond as he quickly took off his old trousers.

"I hope she does," said Tod. "Let's see." He knelt down and checked their length. "I think you might need a shorter inside leg."

"No, they're perfect," said Raymond. "They're sound. Thanks a million."

"No problem." He fixed the laces in the trainers. "Try these on. I'm not looking promotion, so I'm not," he smiled, looking up. "Not half."

"Ball-licking doesn't work with me," said Raymond, smiling.

"I know. You're a straight beam." You've very little, thought Tod, as he rose from the floor. Nothing to show for your years and I don't know how you've done it. "You're a good guy. Whereas, I'm a raker," said Tod, shuddering and thinking how stupid he had been the night before when he had tried to get off with Tina.

"I appreciate what you've just said. I know I upset you a few weeks back by ordering everybody out of the house after your arrest. As if you weren't to be trusted. But I'd have done the same had it been Bobby."

"I know. I know," said Tod, who had been hurt but who understood.

"And, by the way, Tod, you're no raker. I was like you years ago. Loved drinking, loved the girls . . . fuck, it looks like I'm getting back into the drinking! No. Not really.

"Drew the line at dancing, though! But in jail I did a lot of thinking, got everything into proportion. Not that everything's a bed of roses now. I don't do enough for Róisín. Between you and me we haven't even been talking much for the past two weeks. In fact, we're not talking at the moment, which is why I slept on Chrissie's sofa. Róisín wants me to take time off and get some money together but I can't."

"Why not?"

"Why not? Tod, I think about the army twenty-four hours a day. I wake up in a cold sweat in the middle of the night thinking about operations. I go over and over every scenario, everything that can go wrong on a job, ways of getting in and out of places without losing any of you . . . Sorry. I'm not saying you don't think about the 'RA – "

" – No, I know what you mean. It's horses for courses. I know my part. I like a few bob to do a bet. I've expensive tastes," he smiled.

"How does Sal cope?"

"Sal? God, I don't know. She never complains but she's a bit nervous. She just dotes on Nuala. That child's made her life. She's so cute and bright for her age."

Raymond was envious. He and Aidan had formed a powerful bond but he still longed for a child with Róisín. On medical advice she had had to go off the pill for a while and her periods were erratic. When she missed one he was excited at the possibility but she was usually bad-tempered.

They heard the creak of brakes being suddenly applied. Raymond rose and looked out the window. Jeeps had come to a halt outside. Soldiers and policemen climbed out, came up the path but then turned back. It was the house next door they should have been at.

"Wonder is it just a fine or something?" said Tod.

"Could be."

"Well, one thing's for sure."

"What's that?" said Raymond.

"There's no way am I getting into the back of an army jeep with you with that moustache. It's fucking awful."

"Doesn't match my new shirt, then?"

"I'm not even going to answer that. Get it off."

"Thomas."

"What is it?"

"You haven't been to see your mammy and daddy in over two weeks."

"I did. I saw them last Saturday."

"No, you didn't. I was over last Saturday. You had a meeting or something."

"Oh. Well then, I suppose we should all go over today, seeing you're thick with them."

Sal smiled. She got on well with Tod's family. Tod's father, Seamus, adored Nuala and would dandle her on his knee while she nattered away and asked a hundred questions. And Tod's mother, whom Sal still referred to as "Mrs. Malone," out of a deference she thought the woman appreciated, had taken Sal into her confidence about family matters which bespoke a trust that made Sal feel privileged.

When they arrived at the house Mrs. Malone was out in the

kitchen, at the sink, peeling potatoes. Nuala ran straight towards her and grabbed her by the behind, under the skirt, and squeezed. Mrs. Malone shrieked.

"Mother of God, what are you doing, child!" she said.

"Nuala!" shouted Tod. But the child was unintimidated.

"My daddy does that to my mammy," said Nuala, proudly.

"Isn't that interesting," said Mrs. Malone, looking at Tod and enjoying his embarrassment. Sal blushed to the roots of her hair but wouldn't call Nuala a fibber as she had always encouraged her to tell the truth.

"Take no heed of her," said Tod, brushing off the matter. "She watches too many videos."

Nuala looked around to see if she could still remain center-stage but things had moved on and Tod was away into the living room, talking to his father about the racing on the television.

"Give the child some sweeties," said Mrs. Malone. "Up there in the cupboard."

Sal reached up, took out a small bag of chocolates and handed them to her daughter. "What do you say?"

"Thank you, Granny." She snatched the bag. Stanza, the dog, hearing the crinkling of the paper, rose from the floor and came over to the child, wagging his tail.

Nuala had always heard Stanza called "good dog" and still thought that that was his name. Stanza stole a sweet from between Nuala's fingers.

"Bad good dog!" she shouted. "Bad good dog!"

"Stanza!" shouted Mrs. Malone. "Get away, get away!"

Nuala went racing into the living room shouting, "Granda! Granda!", then jumped up on his knee in a reckless manner as if she couldn't care if he caught her or not. Mr. Malone pretended to gasp for strength immediately after taking her securely in his lap and telling her how big she was getting.

Tod sat down, became engrossed in the race and told Nuala to keep quiet.

"Why are they doing that, granda?" she asked.

"Doing what?"

She climbed down off his knee, went to the TV and pointed. "That there?"

"Nuala, get out of the way," said Tod.

"Doing what?" asked her grandfather again.

"That there."

"She means, putting them in the stalls," said Tod.

"Oh, that," said Mr. Malone. "That's so that they don't run backwards."

"It's *not*," she said, jutting out her chin, emphasizing the last word.

"Don't you be cheeky," said Tod.

"When's granda going to die?"

"Any minute now, if you don't shut up," said Tod.

She ran, bouncing, out to the kitchen where Sal and her granny were talking, and asked her grandmother for a drink. She took possession of half a glass of orange juice which she carefully carried back into the living room, one hand around the rim, the other palm supporting the base of the glass. Before she touched it she offered a share to her grandfather, then her father. Then she took a sip.

"Baffroom, Daddy. Baffroom!"

"Wait till this race is over."

"Take her up. I'll tell you who won," said Mr. Malone.

10

EVEN ON DAYS WHEN Róisín knew that the post couldn't possibly include her results she approached the hall with trepidation, only to turn back into the living room not with relief but anger at everything and everyone. Aidan would watch her push back a wisp of hair with unnecessary force, sensed the edge to her breathing. He learnt to take himself off early and bottle up his own sadness at his mother's strange ways.

Raymond was across the border on business when the envelope finally arrived, the arrival itself being the point at which she conceded, without even opening it, what she knew all along – that she had failed. She threw it in the wastepaper basket and immediately felt better. Despite the day being gloriously bright and warm she ran herself a very hot bath, climbed in and reprised her life, feeling she had wasted the last few years. She remembered what it had been like before, on her own, Aidan being taken away for the weekend, she being left free to do as she pleased. The single life had been a simple life and the occasional loneliness she could now compare to an occupational hazard, like catching a cold. She rubbed her neck hard with the flannel. What would have happened had Raymond not knocked on her door that day, coming to apologize for having fought with "her" at his getting-out party? Would she have met someone else, someone that would have made her feel secure and given her real comfort and trust?

She raised her buttocks and lathered her pubic region, thinking of Micky. She had heard that he and his wife Alice hadn't been getting on. She wondered if he ever thought of her or felt regret. After Micky and Alice had had a daughter he saw less of Aidan but in recent months he had resumed weekly contact and sometimes idled on the telephone with her, imparting gossip about mutual friends. Immediately after such calls she felt elation but it quickly turned to simply marvelling at how many times one's ego could engage in self-deception. She had never expected Micky to do to her what he did so she mustn't really have known him. Did she really know Raymond? She shook her head in disbelief as she thought about all the pain those two men had caused her – Micky's affairs with women, Raymond's infatuation with guns and bombs and his obsession with Brits this and 'RA that, with the TV news, the radio news, the newspapers.

Suddenly she remembered the envelope downstairs and how she had invested so much hope in the piece of paper it contained, how those results represented three years of her life, including major disruptions, among which she now included the prolonged farce of marriage.

A few days earlier she had listened to and, despite her glum mood, found herself at first laughing at, then pitying, a man on the radio taking part in the "60-second Quiz." Fairly simple questions would be asked of contestants so that they would score high, feel relaxed and enjoy themselves.

"What did Little Bo Peep lose?" asked the host.

"I don't know what you mean," said the contestant. "Could you repeat the question?"

"How many counties are there in Ireland?"

"Twenty-six, is there?"

"I think the question means, all of Ireland."

"Eh, twenty-eight?"

"What's grown in Paddy fields?"

"It's on the tip of my tongue . . . No, it's gone."

And so on and so forth until the buzzer rang and the clearly embarrassed host declared, "Well, Kevin, you didn't do so good there. Out of ten questions you had no right answers. Never mind. Better luck next time."

"Oh well," replied the man resignedly, and Róisín felt mortified for him even though he indicated no sense of humiliation. She wondered if, afterwards, he felt stupid because of his answers and a real fool for placing himself on public record. How did he manage meeting people on the street, friends and relatives, who had witnessed his abysmal performance?

The presence of the envelope downstairs began to gnaw away at her resolve and the silliness of her stance came home to her. People would ask her how she had done. She dried herself, wrapped herself in a big towel and went to the living room. She picked discarded tissue and orange peel off the envelope and lifted it out. She serrated it with her finger but before removing the piece of paper, went to the kitchen and switched on the kettle. She drummed her fingers on the worktop and made an attempt at whistling. The kettle boiled and she made herself coffee, brought her cup into the living room and set it on the hearth. She opened the paper and looked at the results and her heart thumped. She looked at them again and again until she realized they were no mistake. Then she burst into tears and sobbed, saying, "Fuck you, Raymond Massey. Fuck you." She hugged her legs up, clasped her hands around them, and rocked back and forth, cursing Raymond over and over.

Assuming his mother had gone out after her bath Aidan went to the back of the house, climbed over the gate and found the kitchen door unlocked. He roughly pulled open the living room door, thinking he had the house to himself, and startled Róisín.

"What-to-hell are you doing!" she screamed, jumping up

off the sofa and tugging him by the hair. "Why don't you stay out! Stay out! You scared the living daylights out of me!"

He began to cry and she could feel no pity for him.

"Shut up! Shut up!"

He sobbed all the more and she began clouting him around the head until she was exhausted and he fell down in the corner like a rag doll.

She burst into tears and knelt down on the floor, showering him with wet kisses. He couldn't understand what he had done wrong and he hated her and the way she was always shouting at him and Raymond.

"No wonder Daddy left you," he cried.

The injustice of the remark renewed her temper and she grabbed his T-shirt at the throat. He looked at her so defiantly that she loosened her grip.

"I'm gonna report you to the RS . . . PC . . . A, so I am," he said, as tears once again drowned his vision and his shoulders shook.

"Oh Aidan, Aidan, Aidan. I'm so sorry. Won't you forgive me. . ." She held his hand and rubbed it as if to shine it with love, but there was little response and she was upset that this his first streak of independence should have been debited against their relationship.

The front door was rapped. She looked at her son.

"I'm not going out," he said, before jumping up and running up the stairs. The rapping was persistent.

Róisín shouted, "Who's there?"

"It's Joey. Is Aidan coming?"

She wiped her eyes and opened the door. "Coming where?"

"Summer scheme in the leisure center. We're going to watch canoeing! Over at the Lagan!" said the excited child.

"How much is it?"

"Only £1.50. Tell him to hurry up, the bus is going soon!"

She told Joey to wait and went upstairs. Aidan lay on top of the bed, facing the wall. She sat beside him.

"Aidan? Won't you forgive your mammy? Didn't I forgive you when you lost your birthday watch? And when you didn't come in on time the other night? I'm sorry. Mammy's sorry."

He rolled over and looked at her and she held out her hand. He took it.

"Okay. You want to go to the summer scheme?"

He nodded his head.

"Then come on downstairs and I'll give you the money."

He went off, seemingly unscathed. When she thought about his RSPCA comment she laughed, then she bit her lip.

The telephone rang for the third or fourth time that morning and she continued to ignore it. At lunchtime she poured herself a glass of wine. A good result would have been her ticket to a full-time place at college, a small grant, new faces and friends, fresh views, new outlooks, challenging ideas, a life no longer as a satellite to Raymond.

She was disappointed and ashamed in equal measure. Her anger flared afresh and reached new heights of hatred. She knew she could have done better without her millstone of a husband around her neck. "Useless around the house, useless as a friend, useless in fucking bed!" she said aloud, realizing that she was actually beginning to shout.

She poured herself another glass of wine.

She was still sitting around in her dressing gown when the phone rang again, this time persistently. She answered. It was her mother.

"Well, are you pleased?"

"Ye-yes," she said. "Given the circumstances, two Bs is far better than what I expected." As soon as she lied she regretted it. A lie was like a stone cast into a pond: you could never retrieve the ripples. Her mother would tell her sisters, who'd tell their friends. She tried to rescue the situation but her mother never let up.

"We are so proud of you. Call over. We've a card and a wee present. I was phoning earlier but there was no answer."

"Oh, I was down at the college, getting some forms."

"The dust'll never settle on you," laughed Mrs. Reynolds. "In right away! We'll see you later?"

"Yeah. Yes."

"Have you anything planned?"

She suddenly remembered. "I was to see some girls from the college, around seven," she said, deciding on the spur of the moment that she would drink her results away.

"Well then. Just leave Aidan over here, if you want to make a night of it, or is Raymond around?"

"He's away but is doing his best to get back and let me out."

"Do you think he'll be home on time?"

"I don't think so. It would be great if you could take Aidan . . . Could he get his dinner there?"

"Of course he can. But you're going to call in with him, aren't you, before you go out?"

"Yes, sure. See you later, then."

"Okay, Róisín. And congratulations again. Hold on, hold on! Your daddy wants a word."

"Well done, Róisín. I knew you'd do well. We are very proud of you. Obviously you take it after me," he joked, and Róisín could hear her mother in the background saying, "Would you listen to that."

She laughed with her mother, then took another swig of wine and said goodbye. Had Raymond been in her shoes he wouldn't have lied, would have faced the music. She suddenly despised his integrity because his integrity and pursuits were the father of her disgrace.

She rose, and on her way to the kitchen brushed against the door frame lightly with the abandonment of the slightly drunk. She couldn't face dinner so instead ate some cheese and crackers.

By the time she was ready to go to her parents she had finished the bottle of wine. When she had applied her eye make-up she stared mistily into the mirror. "Do you look drunk?"

she asked herself. "Dunno, but you bloody well feel it! . . . Oh yes, go away this world, go away."

Aidan hadn't come back but she left a message for him to go to his granny's. In her mother's she talked too much and they knew she'd been drinking. She opened her parents' card and when a hundred pounds spilled out her eyes filled and she kissed them. She hurried through the place and when she was gone Mrs. Reynolds remarked, "There's something wrong with her. I hope she's okay."

"She'll be all right. She's just had a few glasses of wine, that's all."

Róisín had never confided in her mother, nor in Lilian, the sister to whom she was closest, that she and Raymond hadn't been getting on, nor that she was incredibly unhappy, but they both knew. They knew by her demeanor, her false enthusiasm, by the weight she'd lost, by her protectiveness and all the gratuitous little things she said, painting up substance around a ghost.

She escaped her parents and took a private taxi into town where she met four of her college friends, two of whom were Protestants and had no idea of the lifestyle Róisín led. Even with wine in her she still found it difficult to lie. One of her company, Janice, was enjoying the evening even though she had done poorly. Through the growing fug, Róisín admired her and wished she had simply told the truth. Fortunately, the subject of the results was quickly exhausted and matters turned to clothes and children and relationships and sex, though never politics. Someone suggested they go off to a disco and Róisín was vaguely aware of Janice dropping out after about an hour. The remaining four were drunk and two of the four had been up dancing with the same two men for some time, leaving Róisín alone with the last young woman, Geraldine, who, like Róisín, was married.

"Róisín. Are you okay? You're fairly gone, aren't you? Do you want me to take you home?" she asked.

"Naw, naw, naw," she replied. "I'm okay. Just a bit sloshed, that's all." She went to lift a glass half-full of red wine but had to drag it across the table. When it came over the edge its weight took effect but she allowed for the dip and raised the glass to her mouth, fairly gracefully, she thought, and felt she was still in control. Soon her two dancing friends returned to ask if they minded them going off with the two men.

"Nottt atall," slurred Róisín. "Enjoy yourselves. You did well today. You deserve it."

"I shall have to be going as well," said Geraldine. "Come on and we'll get a taxi together."

"No, no," said Róisín. "That's only dragging you out of your way." Geraldine lived in the north of the city. "No. I'll walk around to Castle Street and get a black taxi there."

"Are you really sure because there's a taxi firm next door to here."

"Yes, yes. I'm certain. The air'll do me good."

Outside, Geraldine reluctantly let her go off on her own but felt reassured when she saw that Róisín still had a firm step.

Róisín wasn't long in the open air when her inner voice resumed talking in her head and she became unsteady, as if Siamese twins were disputing the direction of their walk.

Massey, you bastard. Your fucking IRA meetings, your fucking IRA life. She suddenly wondered if at the disco she had kissed a man in the corridor to the lady's toilet. She concentrated her thoughts and realized that it had happened and that she had closed her eyes, enjoyed it and smiled when he stepped back to allow her on her way. One of those impulsive incidents between drunk people. When she came out of the lady's room he was gone. But it had happened! She giggled. Bad girl. What are you? A bad girl! Walking through Queen Street she tried unsuccessfully to visualize the man who had kissed her. She practised half-opening her lips and closing her eyes and laughed into herself.

Raymond bottled up his frustration at Róisín's ongoing coolness. He didn't feel that there was anyone he could really confide in. On the train, returning from Dublin, he broached the subject with Bobby, who again sided with Róisín, saying that Raymond should give her more of his time, the way he had devoted more attention to Patricia. Raymond said he was trying and had a holiday surprise for her.

He also regretted conveying some of his woes to Tod: the implicit admission that he wasn't just as in control of his life as he was his life's purpose; that like everyone else he was beset with personal problems. He wished Róisín would accept him for what he was and recognize that outside of republican time he was all hers.

The two men came out of the railway station but there was no sign of Tod.

"You definitely told him which train?"

"Yes," said Bobby. "Maybe there's checkpoints or something."

"He should have been here. I don't like waiting around this place."

"There's a bus goes to the city center. Or we could walk."

"We'll get the bus. I don't want to be seen walking with you," he joked.

"You're a scream. It's you's the red light."

The drop bars weren't on the front door and Raymond thought that Róisín had gone out. But around the living room and on the stairs was a trail of clothes and down beside the sofa was her handbag. And an empty wine bottle. He picked up a piece of scrap paper from the floor: it was her results. He had forgotten about them being due. He read them and sighed, dreaded facing her but knew he must. He climbed the stairs, not knowing what to expect. She lay still in the bed. He ran around to her side of the bed and saw that she was staring at the wall. Although he blew out a loud "phew" she ignored his presence. Beside the bed was a glass, a quarter full of water. He remembered her squirting water into his mouth when years ago they had made love: a country away now.

"I'm sorry about the results."

She quickly turned to face him with a look of surprise or shock. "How do you know? Who told you?"

"They're on the floor."

"Oh." Her head rolled back again on the pillow.

"Can I get you something?"

"Yeah, a shotgun." She was trembling.

"Come on, Róisín, it's not that bad."

"Isn't it. Yesterday I told everybody I passed."

"Sorry? What did you say?"

"You heard me right."

"What did you do that for?"

She turned in his direction again. "Because I was ashamed at having failed, that's why."

"Oh Róisín, I'm so sorry."

"Yes. Well."

"Where's Aidan?"

"Over at my mom's."

"Who all did you tell?"

"My mom and daddy, those that were in my class. . ."

"Won't they find out?"

"They will today when I tell them the truth. That I'm schizophrenic. . ."

He leaned over and kissed her but her lips were shrivelled, had no life. She had the smell of drink dying within her. Something big was on her mind. He looked into her beseechful, almost penitent eyes, but she was beyond his comprehension.

"Raymond, I loved you, you know that, don't you?"

"I know you love me. I love you too," he said, believing that this was merely a routine crisis.

"Don't say that. Please don't say that. You've no idea of the pain you cause me saying that."

"But it's true, Róisín. It's true. Christ, you used to dare me to say it! Remember?"

The cover had fallen from her shoulders, revealing a glimpse of bare breast. Yet rather than simply desirable he still imagined her innocent and vulnerable, the way she had appeared when he first fell for her. He wanted to please her, to take her out of her misery. He kissed her on the neck, as she used to ask him to do, and he thought he heard a gurgle of pleasure in her throat, though it could have been a note of irritation. He stroked her cheek and she closed her eyes as if she could find solace in these few caresses or else couldn't bear to look at him.

There was something changed about her.

"Mind if I get in?" he whispered. "It's been a while, hasn't it?"

She opened her eyes and he saw hesitation or deep pain. She began to tremble, as if the act of making love would begin the same old cycle all over again. She seemed reluctant but nodded and pulled down the cover to let him slide in beside her. He kicked off his shoes, slipped off his jeans but kept on his shirt. When he made love to her she seemed to be miles away. He rolled on to his back and then asked her about the day before. She sketched it out as quickly as she could, mentioning the wine, omitting her fight with Aidan, telling him about the money her parents gave her. She glossed over the events of the evening and said that yesterday was one day she preferred to put behind her and never discuss again.

"Poor Róisín," he said. "Poor Róisín."

Suddenly, she drew away from him.

"Don't 'poor' me, Raymond. I think I've had enough patronizing, if you don't mind." There was an air of aggression to her statement. He was confused. She rolled back over to the way he had found her, as if the last ten minutes or so had been a mere parley in a battle, a time for each side to collect its wounded and dead before resuming hostilities.

He pulled on his jeans. I'll never understand women, he thought. However, he still hoped to lift her spirits. He again lay down beside her.

"I've a house booked in Bundoran for a week," he said, feeling that this moment was as right as he'd ever get it. She made no comment. "It was a wee surprise."

"Where did you get the money?" Again there was hostility in her voice and the question suggested that there were new, higher standards of proofs in their lives. Her back was turned away from him.

"Not to worry about that. It's not a debt."

"Not a debt? I doubt it. But thank you, I don't want to go." She rolled over to face him. "You can take Bobby, if you like."

Raymond was stung. He had gone to considerable trouble to get the money and to get the house. He thought it would please her and take the pressure off them both. A business friend of the IRA also offered him money to help to redecorate the house. He was keeping that surprise in reserve but her attitude had destroyed the joy of giving.

"Are you saying you're not going to go on holiday with me after all the moaning you've done, about not seeing enough of me, about exams, about the house getting you down?"

"That's right."

"You're one selfish bitch, do you know that!"

"I'm a selfish bitch? Are you for real? . . . Get out of this bed, get away from me!" she screamed and began to kick Raymond who was once again astonished at her violence. It wasn't *all* his fault, he thought.

"You are schizoid! You know that!" he shouted into her face before leaving the room.

"Bastard!" she said. "*Murdering* bastard!" she shouted after him.

He turned on the stairs, his face purple, and raced back to her, pulled the duvet off, grabbed and twisted her ankle. She held on to the bedpost but he trailed her out of bed, causing her head to bounce off the floor.

"Never call me a murderer, do you hear! Never!"

She was crying and pulled a sheet over herself. He stormed downstairs, his thoughts all over the place, and she shouted after him, "Murderer! Murderer! Murderer!"

This time he didn't respond but she could hear him swearing and cursing and circling the room like a trapped, buzzing bluebottle. "A fucking madwoman. A fucking madwoman. I married a fucking fruitcake!" Screaming up at the ceiling he continued, "No wonder Micky left you! You must have seen me coming! Fucking damaged goods!" The poison poured out of him.

Róisín pulled on a housecoat, jumped stairs, found him in the middle of the room, rushed up to him and began pummelling his chest, then tried to scratch his eyes. He threw her on to the sofa but she leaped up as if scalded and ran to the kitchen. He heard the cutlery drawer being plundered and it dawned on him what she was after. She emerged from the kitchen with the carving knife.

"Who's a fucking madwoman, eh!" she screamed and jabbed at him. "Who's fucking mad!"

He put his arms out to entreat calm and advise care, but she poked the knife at him and he retreated until his back was against the wall. For a split second he noted that she'd had her hair cut, by quite a few inches.

"I'm a 'nutcase' and you're a murderer. Isn't it as well we never had a baby," she snarled at him.

"I told you not to call me a murderer, now stop it."

"Murderer . . . ," she jabbed him with the knife. "Murderer . . . Murderer!"

Suddenly, he wondered what he had ever seen in her. He loathed her. She was pathetic. She was ugly. Blue veins sat out on her forehead. Her face was flushed red and he could smell her sweat, which struck him as being heavy and sickly. Despite the knife at his stomach he wanted to say something cruel, something that would run to her core, that would shatter her confidence . . . anything . . .

"Look at you!" he crowed. "A madwoman or what! Look at you. You look as if . . . as if you're on the verge of an orgasm with that face of yours. . ." No sooner had he said it than he realized just how pathetic it must have sounded.

"An orgasm? How-to-fuck would you know anything about orgasms," she laughed, hysterically. "I had to fake most of them . . . you *wanker*!" The last word she delivered seethingly. She gave gesture to the knife and he sucked in his stomach and felt a sharp stitch.

He looked into her eyes as if searching for the excitement, the joy, the old affection that their togetherness once granted. But he could see only a murdering capacity that he had provoked.

"I'm sorry," he whispered, and felt the sting of tears at the back of his throat.

"That it's come to this, so am I," she said.

11

"GROWING A BEARD?"

"He wishes he was back on the blanket," said Bobby to Tina, answering for Raymond.

Raymond looked at his watch. "Where-to-hell's Tod? He hasn't been about in a week."

"He'll not be here," said Tina. "The man's dying."

"He was stopped for an hour on the Grosvenor the other day. That's why he didn't pick us up," said Bobby.

"And today he's in bed with a serious asthmatic attack," continued Tina. "And you look as if you should be in bed with him."

"I know. I'm exhausted," said Raymond. "But if I do lie in bed I only become more restless . . . Well, poor Tod. Okay, let's get down to business. The three Branchmen from England."

"I thought you drew a blank," said Bobby.

"Originally. But they're now located. They were away in London. They'll be back this weekend. The house is over by Newforge. I wanted Tod to borrow a car so that I could familiarize you with the layout," he said to Bobby. "If he's not better by the weekend we'll use Pat. The O'Neills can make up the charge. About five pounds of gelly, or mix, if we have to."

Tod breathed with difficulty, as if he was inhaling through a straw and exhaling through a sponge. Every few minutes he coughed up phlegm.

"Here you are," said Sal. "Sit up." She placed a glass of water and two tablets down on the bedside locker and propped up his back. She picked up the tablets and dropped them into the palm of his hand.

He put them to his mouth and washed them down. "Thanks, nurse."

"Well, it's nice to be looked after."

"It just came on me all of a sudden."

"It's stress. The doctor said so the last time." She fixed the quilt around the bottom corners of the bed, then smoothed out a patch beside him for her seat. For a second or two she was anxious because of the way he was looking into her eyes that he was going to confess something or ask her if she was happy and that the conversation would be the prelude to some traumatic upheaval.

"How are you?" he said.

"I'm great. But there's something up, isn't there?"

"No. Why should anything be up?" He wondered if the innermost perpetual screening of his latest sin was apparent to her in some intuitive way.

"That's okay. I thought you were going to tell me something that would make me very sad or unhappy."

Tod blushed but it coincided with a fresh bout of coughing, during which she rubbed and patted his back.

To Bobby Quinn's disgust, Tod had once flippantly pronounced his attitude to women: "Treat them mean, keep them keen." And at a dance just two or three weeks earlier he had made drunken overtures to Tina. She had been with an IRA man from Ardoyne, Gerry Kerr he thought was his name.

"You and Gerry?" he said to her mischievously, when the man went off to the toilet.

"What *are* you talking about?"

"Two-timing Joe?"

"Tod, not everybody's like you. You can't even get your facts right."

"So. If you're not two-timing Joe, would you like to? . . . Take me home, Tina. Away from all this."

"Do you want to go home, Tod?" she said. "Because if you do I'll take you."

"Aye, home with you," he laughed.

"Take yourself off, Tod. You are a disgrace. Do you know that?"

"I suppose you'll be telling Sal you saw me?"

"No, I'll not. She's suffering enough," said Tina.

Tod had relied on such silences. The risk of discovery was always greatest in the immediate aftermath of infidelity, should a loyal friend or relative of Sal witness it and inform on him. He was less vulnerable with the passage of time: one's confidence increased, one could brush memory aside, brush aside the credibility of the informer and rewrite the past, sometimes with a conviction that was startling. But now he lay wretched with failure, struggling to remaster that art, to rewrite memory and relieve himself of the pain and fear that were haunting his every waking moment. He wanted to leave the past behind. He wanted peace. He wanted to look the living in the eye and impart a trust and an assurance: he would never again have hand or part in the taking of human life. He would never again be unfaithful to Sal.

Once, just once, Sal had asked him about a particular woman whose house he had been reported emerging from in the early hours. He denied absolutely that it was him. Then, with a snap of his fingers, he said he knew what the explanation was. He had been seen coming out of a supporter's house, close by, that shared the same exit. That was it. That's what someone saw.

Looking back now on such episodes and the hypocritical rush of affection he had felt for Sal when she seized on his denials with visible relief, he felt disgust and shame.

I am such a shit, he thought.

Sal smiled at him. "Feeling better? I thought you were never going to stop coughing."

"Yeah, I'm a bloody nuisance. Sorry about this."

"It's no bother. I like looking after you. How's your appetite?"

"Not great. Just make for you and Nuala. Where is she?"

"Downstairs, going through those books your mammy got her. There's no doubt about it, she's got your brains."

"Well, let's hope she has her mammy's character . . . ," he said.

"Certainly not her grandfather's."

"What do you mean?"

"My da's."

"What do you mean?"

"Well, he didn't remember her birthday, did he?" she said. "Didn't show up at her christening, never sent us a Christmas card. And look what he did on my mammy, leaving her like that. What chance has she now? None. No wonder she gets on the way she does."

Tod again wondered if there was a subtext to Sal's comments but as usual she was speaking plain.

"You might have no appetite but I think you should drink something. Would you take a cup of tea?"

"Okay, love. I'll have a cup of tea . . . And Sal. Thanks for looking after me."

"You deserve it," she said and smiled back.

I wish I did, he thought. The things I have done on this good, good girl. Would I have been the way I am, regardless of what turn my life had taken? He remembered how ambitious he had been just four or five years before, looking forward to the prospect of his own business, being master of his future. Then he had become emotionally embroiled in the political conflict; then, through Raymond Massey, came involvement with the IRA and his discovery that being so close to death, with its heightened sense of mortality and delusive sense of immortality, being so close to death in the inflicting and surviving, had accentuated his lust for life. The girls I attracted. Did they really fancy me or was it the aura of the IRA that they found exciting? What does it matter now, I am sick of it all. I wasn't cut out for this type of life, and this war's never going to end. It's never going to end. I've been wasting my time. We've all been wasting our time.

He'd made many, many enemies – mostly outside, but some within the IRA – in the past few years. Would they come for revenge if they thought he no longer had authority behind him? But the IRA would still be there. Could he still call on it? Would it act on his behalf? He knew from experience that Volunteers who suddenly walked away were rightly viewed with suspicion. Volunteers who left because of disillusionment were also likely to be treated with disdain for giving up the fight.

Well, I'll just have to live with that contempt, he thought. I've been guilty of it myself. He remembered Jimpy. Jimpy had left the IRA after accidentally killing two civilians. He had gone on the drink and would come into the pub and join a table of former comrades uninvited, the only people he could confide in, and then he would whisper about the dead trying to come up the stairs in the night and him having to keep the lights on. His very demeanor unnerved Tod: the jacket spattered in food droolings, the collar turned up but standing limply around the rinds of his straggly hair, and that slightly hysterical laugh of his. Jokingly, Tod had proposed to Raymond that they shoot him and put him out of his misery but Raymond thoroughly rounded on Tod, saying that Jimpy had been a good republican and needed professional help but couldn't seek it without jeopardizing himself and others.

Tod rolled over on his side and removed one of the pillows that had been propping him. I'd never go that way. Thank God, I've some strength. But I have to get out of the IRA.

Perhaps Sal and I should move across the border or I should go away and work for a few months to get money together. He had heard that there was plenty of work in Germany: good money to be had. I'm lucky, really lucky. I'm still alive. Imagine if I had reached this conclusion in jail and I was doing twenty years. I'd be shattered. Then he thought about the hunger strikers and he was overwhelmed with feelings of guilt. What those men came through for their beliefs I could never have done. Yet they inspired me. Their greatness, their selflessness.

Give yourself a shake, Tod, he said to himself. *This* has never been you.

Was I false all along? The bombings and the shootings – did they mean *anything*? At the time. At the time, yes. But I should recognize the truth. This life is not for me and I am unworthy of the task. He realized that his breathing was much more relaxed and he felt much brighter. He thought of the future. I could be somebody. I *can* give Sal and Nuala a future!

Reality galloped up and overtook his reverie, scattering his dreams in a cloud of dust. How can I simply walk away? But how can I simply continue as if nothing has changed inside me? I can't go on like this, I can't! His wheezing returned and he coughed to dislodge a gob of ticklish phlegm enmeshed deep in his lung. He had a fit of prolonged coughing but brought up nothing but the bitter taste of salt. That's it, punish me, God. I deserve it, after all the hurt I've caused. I'm a disgrace to my friends and comrades. Comrade? Some comrade I've turned out.

He thought of Raymond and he was brought low with a guilt as great as that caused by his darkest deeds or his disloyalty to Sal or his breach with his ideals. Raymond towered over him more than ever: his consistency, integrity, resolve, commitment. His sacrifices.

I am not fit to tie his laces.

He heard Sal's steps on the stairs. She came into the room

with his tea. "There you are." There was a sandwich on a plate.

"I'll never eat that, love."

"Well, Thomas, you'll just have to try. For me?"

"I'll see."

"There's the door," she said. She looked out the window. "It's Raymond."

"Raymond! What's he want? Sal, tell him I'm asleep, tell him I'm too sick to see anybody. Won't you, won't you?" Tod felt nauseous and his temperature suddenly soared.

Sal was surprised at his vehemence but was pleased that he'd put her in charge. She went to the door. A few seconds later Raymond's voice and laugh boomed in the living room below. Tod wondered if he was staying for a cup of tea but then he heard their voices in the hall and the front door close. Sal came up the stairs.

"Well?"

"He just called in to see how the invalid was and he left in some money."

"Oh, right," said Tod, relieved. "I'd forgotten about that money. For petrol." The irony of Raymond paying for his petrol triggered another bout of guilt.

"I told him you'd be out of it for a few more days. He says not to worry. I have to say, although he was laughing, he looked dreadful. Has an awful beard. He said you can get him through Chrissie's."

Through Chrissie's, thought Tod. That means he's out of the house again. They've been fighting again. He put down his cup.

"What's wrong?"

"I'm sorry but I can't even drink this."

"I want to get the doctor."

"I don't need the doctor. I just need peace. Peace and rest. Sal?"

"What, Thomas?"

"I'm thinking of moving. . ."

"Moving? What about Nuala? What about me?" she said, her voice quivering.

"Don't be daft. You'll be with me."

"But what about the movement? Are you leaving it?"

"I think so. I think I've had enough."

"Thomas!" she yelped with delight. "I've been dying to hear that for ages!" She threw her arms around him and he smiled. "My nightmare has always been that you'd be killed and what would I do without you. That's great news. We'll have a new life together, a better life, I promise you!"

Within minutes of her leaving the room the absurdity of his ambitions became stark and he realized that he would always be a Volunteer. But an hour later he could see only one way out of the deteriorating mess that was his life and that was to make the break, to cut the artery that connected him to a struggle which he could no longer participate in.

Lying in bed was driving him crazy. Tomorrow night, Wednesday, he would taxi, whether or not he was fully recovered. At least that would help take his mind off things.

12

"IT'S STARTING TO RAIN," said Pat, as he switched on the wipers. The rubbers dragged themselves shuddering across the windscreen but greased by more rainfall, picked up speed.

"So much for the weather forecast," said Raymond.

"It was predicted," said Bobby. He and Raymond were in dark but not waterproof clothing and wore good boots.

"That's not what you said earlier," said Raymond, smiling at him.

Pat drove through Finaghy, through several residential areas before turning down a long cul de sac. A vehicle came towards them with its lights on full beam but then dipped them. They drove on for another quarter of a mile.

"Here. Just here," said Raymond anxiously.

"It's okay. I know the spot," said Pat. "Take care. I'll see you two in an hour from now if I don't hear from you first. Okay?"

"Okay."

They left the car quickly, quietly closing the doors, leaped over a fence and disappeared into a field. Already they were breathing heavily – but it was just an initial burst of adrenalin. They watched the car proceed on down the lane of mansions and villas and then, a few minutes later, its return as it headed back to the west of the city.

Raymond took the radio from inside his jerkin, switched it on and spoke. "Imagine sending a dog out on a night like this. Keep us a sandwich, Joan, won't you?" he said and feigned a laugh.

After a second or two a reply came back. It was breaking up but they could just make out Tina's voice saying, "Ham and cheese, right?"

"Right," said Raymond. He switched off the radio and wiped off the rain that it had caught.

The two men silently crossed the field and before long their feet were wringing, their boots having offered not enough protection. They climbed over another gate and went around the perimeter of a bowling green. The sky was completely overcast but nature still seemed to shine from some invisible source: the blades of grass glistened and the rustling leaves along the hedgerows gleamed. They found the tow path, got their bearings and after a few minutes scrambled through thick bushes and dry earth and up an embankment. At its top they were surprised at how illuminated was the stretch of open ground before them which led to the back lawns and gardens of private bungalows.

"I thought it would have been darker," whispered Raymond. "It's only one lamp too."

Bobby looked at Raymond and started laughing.

"What's up?" said Raymond. But as soon as he asked the question he knew, with a pleasant helplessness, what they were going to say next.

"You should see the look of you. Your face! It's covered in mud."

"Me? You should see the look of you," said Raymond with a smile.

"Okay, okay," said Bobby. "Now, which house is it?"

"That one over there. I think there's a light lit. The living room's at the back. They must still be up. Maybe they've women in."

"Can we get closer?"

"We're gonna have to but I didn't think it would be so bright at the backs. Hold it. The light's gone out. They must be going to bed. See tomorrow night, we'll come later."

They waited for ten minutes.

"I'll go over and see the lie of the land," said Bobby.

"No. You stay here. I'll go over. I want to see what the back fence is made of, what sort of cutters we'll need."

"You're always 'going over'," said Bobby. "I'll go for a change."

"Well, wait another while."

"Sure, it must be about three now. There's no sign of life."

"Okay," said Raymond. "But be careful."

"Want my chewing gum," said Bobby, popping it out on the end of his tongue.

"Fuck off, you," said Raymond, smiling.

Bobby emerged from the bushes. His feet squelched in his boots as he ducked and weaved in his journey to the backs of the bungalows. He knelt and pulled some ivy aside to examine the wire fencing. He thought he heard a noise some way off, toward a line of trees. Raymond wondered why he had paused and was staring in that direction. Then Raymond saw what Bobby was looking at. Two figures dressed in dark clothing rushed from the trees and raced over to the kneeling man. Bobby leaped to his feet but was punched in the face with some heavy object and stumbled backwards before slipping on the ground with one of his assailants on top. As Raymond scrambled out of the embankment he saw the other figure shoot Bobby in the leg and heard Bobby scream.

A flare exploded overhead and everyone looked up. The falling rain stood still in the air, like the glass beads of a curtain illusively cutting off one space from another.

"There's another one!" screamed one of the men.

Raymond heard the English accent and saw the figure quickly raise the gun and fire a shot in his direction which seemed to trigger a heavy fall of rain. He felt a burn in his arm and dived back into the bushes, rolling over and over, down towards the towpath and bursting through a splintering of branches and ripping of leaves.

He dived into the bramble on the other side and fell for a bit before being stopped by the bough of a tree. The rain was beating off the uppermost leaves, providing some camouflage for his panting.

The sky lit up again. High above he could see several figures, including men in military uniforms, run along the path, before their movements became jerky in the flickering stroboscopic light of a dying flare.

"What's your name? What's your fucking name?" a soldier was shouting at Bobby. "What's your name and we'll get you a medic?"

"What's *your* fucking name!" shouted Bobby.

Raymond then heard a single shot, followed again by raised voices, but this time giving orders or directions. He felt broken but kept repeating, "Think of yourself, think only of yourself." He suddenly realized that the river was directly below him: he hadn't thought it was so close. He slid into its cold waters and though he could touch the bottom the current was deceptive at the edge. His teeth were uncontrollably chattering and he feared the noise could give him away. He hugged the bank and allowed the flow to carry him downstream and away from the commotion.

After what seemed like an age he was out of immediate danger and could see that the helicopter with its searchlight was concentrating on an area some distance away. He was able to wade across the river and climb out. He came up through an alley at the back of a building which was under refurbishment. He climbed over a gate, went through a yard, then over another high gate which led to a main road. There wasn't sight

of vehicle or person but the ground was sleeked with fallen
leaves, some here and there writhing. He found a telephone
box almost immediately and he had no choice but to ring a
number which was probably under tap. For an age no one
answered, then he heard Sal's voice at the other end, speaking
drowsily.

"Hello. What is it, please?"

"Sal? Sal! Put Tod on, please."

"Who is it? What time is it?"

"Sal! I need to speak to Tod!"

"Raymond. Raymond, is that you?" she asked.

He wished she hadn't used his name. "Yes, Sal. It's me.
Please hurry up."

"Thomas. *Thomas* . . . It's Raymond."

"Wha? What?" said Tod, waking up and taking the phone.

"Tod. Tod. I need to be lifted right away. Can you get me
picked up?"

"From your place? Where? Where are you? What's up?"

"I'll tell you later. Do you remember the place you got the
puncture, about two months ago?"

"Eh, I'm thinking."

"It was a Sunday night. We were coming back from the
country."

"Yes. Yes, I remember."

"I'm just up the road from there. On the left-hand side. I'll
be at a telephone box. I'll be back at it in twenty minutes. Can
you organize something?"

"I'll come myself. . ."

"No! No. Somebody different. Clean. Can you do it?"

Raymond sounded desperate.

"You can depend on me," said Tod. "Twenty minutes. Is
everything okay?"

"I'll tell you later. I have to go."

It sounded extremely ominous, thought Tod.

"What's wrong?" said Sal.

"I have to get Raymond a lift. I'll ask Lily Henderson. She's sound."

"But what's wrong?"

"I don't fucking know what's wrong, Sal, okay! I have to go."

"But, Thomas. You told me you were finished."

He withered her with his look.

He had come in early from taxiing and taken a sleeping tablet when he couldn't get over. But its effect had now completely worn off. He was alert and on duty. He was needed.

"Raymond's in trouble, Sal, and I'm the only one can help him. Understand?"

She nodded and got out of bed with him.

Tina arrived first. She entered the kitchen through the back door and nodded to a woman making tea. The woman returned a weak but sympathetic smile and not knowing what to say said nothing.

Tina pushed open the door of the living room and Raymond made to rise from the settee but then saw who it was.

"Don't move," said the nurse, tetchily, as she completed bandaging Raymond's wound. "I really think you should go to the hospital, just in case."

"It's only a graze," he said. "Looks like a knife-wound."

"It'll pass for that," she said, and got up. "Now, don't forget to take these, okay? Two in another three hours, and another two before you go to bed. And I'll see you tomorrow."

"Thanks, again," he said. "I'll see you tomorrow but it'll be somewhere else."

"Okay. He knows where to get me," she said, indicating her brother, the owner of the house, who stood up with her as she prepared to leave. Turning to Tina, her brother said, "Would you like a cup of tea?"

"No, thanks."

"None for me, either," said Raymond.

"Right. I'll leave you two in peace."

As soon as they were gone Tina sat down beside Raymond and put her arm through his. "I'm sure you're shattered."

He nodded.

"Poor Bobby." And as soon as she said his name she felt tears gather.

"It's my fault," said Raymond. "He wanted to carry a short and I said, no, not until the actual job. You know, in case we were stopped at a checkpoint. Had we been armed we'd have had a chance."

"Don't say that. It's not true. It's not your fault. But they knew you'd be there, that's for sure."

"I've racked my brains, Tina, and I can come up with nobody in our squad I don't trust. Even the O'Neill brothers. They're a hundred. We've been so tight. Maybe the Brits have all sorts of houses staked out just on the off-chance."

"Maybe we shouldn't have used the radios or maybe the car that Pat borrowed was known. But at the end of the day I think you were squealed on and everybody is suspect: whoever gave you the info; whoever at BB level cleared the job; me, Pat, and the two O'Neills."

"And me. I sent Bobby to the wire. . ."

"Raymond! Raymond! Snap out of it right now! That's an order," she said, and smiled.

"I've just noticed. You've no make-up on."

"And look what I'm wearing. It all now seems so much nothing," she said.

"What about Pauline, has she been told?"

"She's over with Bobby's parents now. The three of them are just sitting in the living room crying non-stop, along with Bobby's sisters. His kid sister Deirdre is taking it the worst. They'll be getting the body in the afternoon, provided there's no messing about."

"If they mess about," said Raymond, grimly, "I'll bomb the next RUC man's funeral and fuck them."

He sat staring into the empty fireplace. Tina didn't contradict him.

"I'll have to contact Róisín. There'll be all sorts of rumors doing the rounds. She'll be worried sick."

"I've already sent word. Pat's bringing her over here in about ten minutes. She wants to see you."

"How did she find out?"

"A woman's instinct. She was knocking on Chrissie's at half seven this morning, asking her did she know where you were or where you'd stayed last night."

"Fuckin' Bobby," he said, as if he hadn't heard her. "Poor Bobby . . . When did you say Róisín was coming over?"

"She'll be here any minute. How long has it been since you saw her?"

"Six or seven days. We'd a huge fight. Did the Brits raid?"

"No, but it's early yet."

"I don't think they knew who Bobby was."

"They know now and they knew then."

"The Brit shouted, 'There's the other one!' or 'There's another one!' Jesus, I wish I knew for certain. It makes all the difference."

The living room door opened and Pat led Róisín in. Raymond stood up to greet his wife. She crossed the room hurriedly and put her arms around him.

"I'm sorry, so sorry, Raymond. Bobby . . . ," she said, and began crying. She felt something, either Raymond wince or the bandage beneath the strange, large shirt he wore. "What's that?"

"Oh, nothing. I hurt myself getting away, that's all."

"Were you shot? Were you! The news is saying that soldiers believe they shot an accomplice."

"No, no, it's just a cut."

"He was grazed," said Tina. "But it's okay."

"Grazed? Raymond, I want you to go to the hospital. An infection could set in. Anything. . ."

"I'm okay," he said. "Really. It's nothing. I've a few stitches and you'd think I had been cut with a knife. Stabbed."

"We're just going out to the hall to have a word," said Tina.

Raymond nodded and Tina and Pat left the couple on their own.

"Look at you," said Róisín. "It took us to split up before you'd grow your beard again."

"I didn't want to split up."

"But we can't live together. You know that. We were ready to kill each other. I respect Bobby and what he lived for and you, but I can't take all that grief, I can't take it."

"Then what did you come around here for?" he said, accusingly.

"Raymond, don't be starting. It's neither the time nor the place."

"Well, it was you who started it. Bobby hardly cold . . . and you on the lecture tour."

"I'm sorry. I shouldn't have said it. I still worry about you, you know. And Aidan wants to know why you haven't been around."

They had sat down on the settee and she linked his good arm, the way Tina had done, and he began to view Róisín slowly with the objectivity of distance. What he did last night he would do again tomorrow. He loved this woman more than he'd loved any woman but he couldn't change the world *and* keep her love. He had known that from the beginning. He should never have tried to occupy both worlds. It was selfish. He loved the man who was dead. The man who when they had him on the ground wounded still defied them.

"Are you going to the funeral?" she asked.

"Yes. Of course. But the beard's coming off."

She wondered for a second if he was being provocative but skipped it. "Do you think there'll be trouble?"

"There's been trouble at all the others."

"I wish you wouldn't," she said.

He felt strong. He gave her one of those looks, suggesting she be serious, deal with the real world, that she wise up.

"Do you want me to go with you?" she asked, surprising him.

"Thanks. Thanks. I really appreciate it but I would only be worried about you, on the lookout for you."

"Well, I'll be watching, then. I'm going to see Pauline now, see if there's anything I can do."

"Don't say what you said to me."

"Of course not. I'm not that stupid."

"I know you're not."

He saw that she meant to kiss him goodbye and he readied himself for a kiss on the lips but she kissed him on the cheek. And despite his strength he felt disappointed.

"Maybe I'll see you at the funeral," he said.

"Okay," she replied and left.

He stared after her and felt some regret.

Tina came back in. "Pat's away to see the brigade about arrangements. You'll need to stay out of Chrissie's, just in case they come looking. Do you want me to get you a billet?"

"No, Tod's fixed me up, thanks. But I'd prefer to get to the wake house and stay there. If it's Pauline's I'd need to go this morning. Her place is hard to get into."

"I think he's being buried from home, his mother's. We'll get you over there later. Meanwhile, have a rest, take a nap."

"I couldn't. Just couldn't."

13

THE UNDERTAKER screwed down the coffin lid. Pauline and Bobby's mother turned to each other and embraced while Mr. Quinn put his arms around both of them. Sal stood crying in the kitchen.

"If anything ever happened to you," she whispered.

"There, there," said Tod, holding her tight. "Bobby was a gentleman. A gentleman." He had said the same to Mr. Quinn when he had first come to offer his condolences.

"Thank you, Tod," Mr. Quinn had replied. "I appreciate it."

When Raymond had arrived back to base Tod learnt at first hand what had happened. Later, at home, suffering from a bad headache, he couldn't get any peace because Nuala was endlessly chattering despite being scolded by Sal, climbing over the settee or expecting Tod to swing her around or carry her on his back. That afternoon Bobby's remains were released from the morgue. Coming out of the hospital the cortège was stopped and split up by the RUC and the hearse was forced to drive to West Belfast in the middle of a convoy of police jeeps.

At the wake Tod approached the coffin with great apprehension but also curiosity. Raymond and he stood there together. He was surprised at how detached he felt. The undertaker, or whoever, had done a miraculous job on Bobby's face. The bruising was conspicuous but the entry wound above his right eye looked like just a little dimple or small indentation. What he saw was the dead husk of a man, as if the real Bobby had irresponsibly vanished without trace leaving behind a shell and all these bewildered relatives and friends.

Upstairs, a few minutes later, Raymond said, "Don't you feel guilty? Just being alive?"

"I know what you mean," said Tod, shaking his head.

They had gathered in the room and talked about the operation that had gone wrong. Tod made Pat repeatedly go over his account of their trip to Newforge and the car which they had met on the lane and his return to West Belfast and whether there was any detail he had forgotten. He irritated Pat so much that Tina had to step in and calm things. Tod asked to be excused. Outside the house stood a large crowd of republican supporters surrounded by a much larger force of RUC men in riot gear. Tod was stopped, searched and verbally abused, and his name and address taken by police as he left.

He went for a long drive at a reckless speed, sometimes at a hundred miles per hour. He thought about Bobby and Raymond and himself, what they'd been through together, yet what wasted lives they had led. He made preposterous speculations about the cause of Bobby's death but settled for the conclusion that at the end of the day Bobby's lifestyle was to blame. Hadn't Raymond often said that the good Volunteer, the real fighter, always gets killed? So, having sorted the problem in his head, Tod drove home to capitalize on his easeful mood. But when he got home Sal told him that Nuala was talking to herself.

"What do you mean?"

"Come and see."

He followed Sal into the living room where Nuala was sitting quietly in a chair. Normally, she would run and greet him.

"How's my pet?"

"Hiya, daddy," she said, before resuming watching television.

"I see nothing wrong," he said to Sal.

"Not now. But just watch."

After five minutes, Nuala turned around and began addressing thin air. "I'll look after you," she said.

"Nuala. Who are you talking to?"

"My friend, daddy."

"What friend?"

"My big brother."

"What? What did you say?"

"I'm talking to my big brother." She turned away. "It's okay. It's my daddy."

"Stop that, Nuala!" shouted Tod. "Stop it, now!" he said, and made a move towards her.

"He's gone away! You've made him run away!" cried Nuala and ran to Sal's side.

Tod was shaken. "I have to go out," he said to Sal, and quickly left. He walked to a club and had a few drinks on his own, staring into his pints. He went home when Nuala was sure to be asleep. Sal asked was he feeling any better and he apologized. It took hours for him to fall over and even then he was disturbed by a nightmare in which a soldier chased him. Tod broke into a house, ran upstairs, climbed into bed and hid underneath the duvet, next to a sleeping woman. But the soldier found him, dragged him out of bed, put a gun to his head and blew his brains out, splattering them across the carpet. Tod jumped up suddenly in the bed, terrifying Sal.

"Oh, Thomas! What's wrong, what's wrong!" she cried.

"A bad dream, just a bad dream," he said, trying to compose himself and interpret its meaning.

"You're really upset and angry about Bobby, aren't you. I've never seen you like this before."

"I'm angry, okay. Fucking Bobby, and the way the cops treated his family. The bastards."

"Thomas, you're still thinking about leaving, aren't you?"
He didn't answer.

"I know how you feel at the minute, but it'll pass. Thomas, I couldn't see you in a coffin like Bobby. It would kill me. Honestly," she said, trembling.

"Sal. Don't. Don't. Not now. We'll talk about it again, okay?"

She nodded but her continued sniffling, an emotional weakness she wore too easily, annoyed him. He lay his head on his pillow and played back the past, the past he had so recently pledged to put away, and wondered what depths he could not plumb. It was thoughts of Jackie Brennan, with another woman's face grafted on to hers, that came to him the easiest: how adventurous Jackie had been in bed, against the wall, on the floor, in the car.

In the car. In the car.

The fucking car.

What a mess. What a fucking mess.

Tod closed his eyes. But he didn't sleep. He thought about the hotel he'd been in on the outskirts of Belfast. How easy it would be to walk into the security hut, arrest the two civilian searchers in their pretentious fucking uniforms, lift the barrier and let the car bomb through to the front door.

That's it, he thought. That's it! He began to feel better. Easy breeze.

Rain poured down on the heads of the mourners gathered in the street and overspilling into the small gardens.

The coffin was brought out of the house, borne on the shoulders of Mr. Quinn and Raymond at the front, and Mrs. Quinn's brother from New York and another relative at the back. It was draped in a tricolor, on top of which were pinned a black beret and a pair of leather gloves.

As soon as the riot police saw the beret and gloves they drew their batons and began forcing their way through the mourners. Mrs. Quinn, seeing the commotion, became hysterical and had to be calmed by her daughters. Fighting erupted in the gardens and there were screams and shouts and cursing until stewards restored calm and the police received orders to settle into their new positions.

"Is there a doctor? We need a doctor!" someone called from a doorway.

"Don't let them provoke you!" shouted a Sinn Féin official, through a loud-hailer. "Stay calm! Stay in your place!"

"Make sure you show this on TV!" screamed a woman at a cameraman and reporters. "Show this, if they let you!"

The mourners made a gap for two priests who went and parleyed with a number of senior RUC officers. They returned and spoke to Sinn Féin officials, one of whom then came up to Mr. Quinn.

"They said they won't let the funeral go ahead with the beret and gloves on top."

"Then back into the house," said Mr. Quinn. Bobby's coffin was taken indoors and the trestles set out again.

Inside the house Mrs. Quinn, still sobbing, was being consoled. "I don't care, Brian. I just want Bobby buried in peace and nobody else killed. I don't care," she repeated, remonstrating with her husband.

Raymond went out to the kitchen to talk to IRA people. "They're starting to argue," he said.

"Well, I hope they don't buckle. The cops have gone buck mad out there," said Seán Brennan. "There's a kid about fourteen away to the hospital. His nose shot off by those pigs. Tod's been hit by a baton and his eye's busted."

"Seán," said Raymond. "Could I see you out the back for a second?"

The two men went into the back garden.

"The family will buckle in a day or two, don't you agree?" said Raymond.

"I think so."

"Let's go along with what the cops are saying, but when we get on to the main road where we have our numbers, then we'll do what *we* want."

"But the family will have to give their word. . ."

"That's okay. Nobody will argue with us at that stage."

"Right. Let's do that."

The RUC agreed to the tricolor on the coffin and a civilian guard of honor and, in return, their men stayed six feet away from the mourners.

The carrying of the coffin was shared in turn by many hundreds of people. Along the main road thousands joined in the funeral so that the RUC were pushed further and further away. Raymond then stepped forward and placed on top of the flag the beret and gloves he had carried in his pocket. The news shot through the crowd, which became ecstatic.

As they approached the republican plot the piper played "The H-Block Song," about the blanket protest and the prisoner refusing to wear the convict's uniform and meekly serve his time, and Raymond remembering his days and nights in prison with his friend suddenly found himself unusually maudlin. In jail the warders never gave them enough to eat. Each morning when the door opened they were served tiny bowls of cornflakes. This particular day it had been Raymond's turn to collect them. He was starving. He picked up the two bowls of cornflakes and spotted that one had a little bit more than the other and handed Bobby the smaller of the two as if he hadn't noticed. Bobby took it, but Raymond knew he'd seen the move. Then Raymond felt guilty and said to Bobby to give him his bowl, his had more, but Bobby said it was okay, he'd plenty.

With a solid mass of people now surrounding the graveside, three masked IRA Volunteers stepped forward and fired a three-volley salute over the coffin. As they disappeared into the crowd there was a huge cheer and prolonged handclapping. There was some scuffling with the riot police on the margins but the crowd held their ground and the police relented.

During the oration Raymond held and squeezed Pauline's hand but he heard not a word of what was said. He stared into the hole in the ground and remembered his promise to Bobby to come back when the British had left.

In Castlereagh the detectives told Raymond they knew that it was he who had been with Bobby and escaped. They made jokes about his "knife" wound.

"We recovered a gun at the scene but there were no finger-prints on it," said the police officer. "Bobby Quinn. A two-time loser. What a dickhead, Davy," he said, laughing.

"You mean, what a stupid, silly-billy, dickheaded, Paddy-fucking-Irishman!" said the other detective.

"Show him the photos."

"Boy like that would only throw up."

"Raymond! Raymie Massey? No way! He loves those pic-tures, but only if the stiffs have no arms or legs or been well-cooked. Especially women and kids."

"Here. Have a look."

They threw down on the table a selection of photographs of Bobby lying dead.

"Squealed like a pig, so he did. 'Please don't shoot! Please don't shoot!'"

"Yellow bastard didn't care who was in his way when he killed."

"'Don't shoot! Please, don't shoot!'"

"Kicking up the daisies now, the stupid fucker."

"Raymond. You just can't win. You just can't win. When will you ever learn?"

"You'll be next. Fucking glory-hunter."

"Discover anything in Castlereagh?"

"No," said Raymond to Pat. "Not a thing."

"Well, we have," said Pat. "When you were away we finally

got checking the car. There was a fucking bugging device under the chassis, built right into it and camouflaged with muck and dirt. First time the guy looked he missed it, but then found it. He removed the power pack, the radio guy took it away for examination. He was fucking lucky. There was a tiny hidden battery and the thing was still transmitting."

"Are you serious?"

"Yip."

"What happened?"

"He hit it with a hammer."

Tina sat in silence.

"But I thought the car was clean. How could the Brits know we were going to use that particular car?" said Raymond, looking at Tod, who shrugged his shoulders.

"That's what we were told," said Pat. "That it was clean. But it turns out it had been used by a unit in the Murph and some of them had been stopped in it. It's a fucking disgrace. A man's life."

"Somebody's head should roll for that. . ."

"It was the owner who said it was clean, just trying to help out, do his best, I guess."

Raymond took a deep breath and sighed. "Well, at least that's a better explanation than a tout."

"I wouldn't rule out a tout just yet," said Tina.

"I know we can't," said Pat, "but the security people have questioned everybody and we're all in the clear. The car must have been traced or followed on the dummy run and from that they worked out the target."

"At half an hour's notice?" said Tina. "I don't think so."

"Well, what do you want to do?" asked Pat. "Stop all operations? We don't even have a suspect, nor one person who was in the know that we can say has been acting strangely."

"I would go along with Tina," said Tod. "You don't know when the bugging device was placed. It could have been attached *after* Bobby's death to cover up for an informer. Nevertheless,

I don't have any other suggestions and I'm anxious to get back
into ops."

"It *is* possible that the device was put there after Bobby was
killed," said Raymond.

"Well," said Pat. "It's up to yourselves. I don't know where
we go from here. We either operate as a unit or break up. I'll
go along with your decision, Raymond."

"Where's the O'Neills?" he asked.

"I wanted this conversation without them," said Pat. "I
didn't tell them."

"Why not?" said Tod.

"Umm . . . I dunno. One day at a time."

14

TINA WALKED THROUGH Turf Lodge towards the lower Glen Road. The night was dark and cold, a harbinger of winter. She thought of next month, her boyfriend Joe's release, their holiday in the sun. "Top of the Pops" had been on the television in the house she had just left, a roaring fire in the grate, kids on the floor doing homework. Before leaving she had checked the contents of her handbag. She again read Joe's letter before tearing it up.

She passed a house where the parlor blinds remained open. Inside, a teenage girl practised at a piano, the soft, warm notes audible through the glass which kept the cold at bay.

Tina's unit had been busy over the past two weeks. They had car-bombed a hotel. The O'Neill brothers had been brought back into the active service unit and had made up a small booby-trap which Pat and Tod placed in a hollowed-out gable wall of a derelict house. On the outside they stuck up a "Brits Out" poster. As expected, a soldier tried to rip it off as a memento. It exploded, injuring him and a colleague.

Tina crossed the Andersonstown Road. A few minutes later she waved down a Twinbrook taxi and boarded. She folded down a seat in the back, next to an adolescent girl in jeans who chewed gum. Opposite them were a middle-aged woman with shopping at her feet, a young man in jacket and overalls, his hands ingrained with dirt from laboring, and a drunk man who asked everyone how they were keeping, before going around them again with the same question, then apologizing for his repetitiveness. Webs of light circulated at different speeds in the dark cab, momentarily revealing the different expressions on the faces of the passengers. Odorous hot air rose from the floor. Rain had begun to fall, gusts of wind smearing it across the windows.

Tina was facing backwards, saw Kennedy Roundabout disappear, then the traffic lights at Finaghy. As the taxi passed Woodburn Barracks a foot patrol was just leaving the base and she looked for a piece of wood to touch. She turned and saw up ahead a policeman step into the middle of the road and wave a red light. Parked at the side were military jeeps. The taxi stopped and another policeman approached to check the driver's documents. Having satisfied himself that they were in order he knocked the windows, indicating that they be pulled down, then he shone his torch in turn on the faces of the passengers. No one took any heed.

"Would you mind stepping out, please," he said. "Everyone."

There was much complaining but all complied, the drunk man having to be helped out by the young laborer. They stood at the side of the road. Tina was concerned that she might be recognized. She hid her nervousness by talking to the lady with the shopping.

"Name, please?" asked a policeman.

"Mrs. Russell."

The soldiers were now carefully examining the taxi: a third had rolled underneath with a torch.

"Could you come over here, please?" The policeman had put the question to the middle-aged woman. She went behind a jeep where a woman PC asked her to open her coat for a search.

Tina's stomach tightened. It was now her turn.

The policewoman apologized for having to do this on a night so bitter. Tina opened her coat.

"What's that?" Her hand had arrived at the bulge beneath Tina's sweater.

"It's what you're looking for."

"Gary! Gary! Quick! She's got a gun! The bitch's got a gun!" The policewoman suddenly backed away, leaving Tina exposed and dangerously compromised. She didn't know what to do with her hands and the gun in her waistband felt like an abominable rat lockjawed to her flesh. Before she could think, she was brought to the ground from behind. Her mane of hair was held tight before she was rolled over onto her back. A policeman pulled the sweater over her head, revealing the butt of a revolver at her waist, her bare stomach and a silk brassiere. He almost ripped the gun from her, then he rose.

"Don't fucking move, you bitch!"

Her hands were bagged and handcuffed before she was hoisted on to her feet.

"Provo groundsheet," grinned the policewoman into her face. "It'll be a long, long time before you're screwed again! Now, what's your name?"

Her life was in two.

15

IT WAS EARLY MORNING. Róisín knocked on the door. She rapped again when no one answered. She was just about to turn around when Sal opened the door. Seeing her at last, Róisín trembled.

"What do *you* want? You've a bloody cheek!"

Róisín hesitated. "Can I come in? I don't want to stand here on the step. I think we need to talk."

Sal turned on her heels and walked up the hall, indifferently. But at least the door hadn't been slammed in her face, thought Róisín, who gingerly stepped into the hall and lifted a coat which lay on the floor. She hung it on a cuphook. The place was a mess and smelt. When Róisín followed Sal into the living room, Nuala ran frightened to her mother and sought refuge in her lap.

"Before you say a word about my Thomas being responsible I want you to know a thing or two. Your husband murdered my Thomas, my child's father. Thomas was innocent, do you hear me? Are you listening! My life is ruined. Ruined. This child's on the phone every night, asking to speak to her daddy up in heaven. She's all I've left. Thomas was not an informer . . . he was not an informer, and you are all bastards, everyone of you . . ." Sal began crying and Nuala wrapped her arms around her neck.

Róisín burst into tears, rose from her chair and rushed to Sal's side. She knelt on the floor and held the younger woman's hand.

"Sal, Sal, you might be right, I don't know, I don't know . . ."

"I *do* know! I do know! He was shot because he wanted to leave the IRA and they wouldn't let him. Because he knew too much. Or else he was shot to cover up for an informer higher up.

"Fifteen people were at his funeral. *Fifteen people!* You've no idea how humiliating it was for me and his family. No idea. No acknowledgement. Nobody to defend him after all he'd given. People crossing to the other side of the street to avoid me. People who you thought were your friends ignoring you. Kids taunting Nuala, a child not even three. A house empty. You've no idea of the pain or the heartache. . ."

"Oh but Sal, I do. I do. I lost my husband as well, you know."

"Don't talk! I know Thomas was no angel. Is that what you've come to tell me? I know he saw somebody else, some hussy. But I loved him, loved him. And he loved me." She rocked back and forth. "And we were going to move away from all this. Get away and start a new life. But you. Your husband wouldn't let him and I'm glad Raymond's dead, I'm glad. But you? You didn't even love your husband. Sure you threw him out. I saw him. I would never have done that to Thomas. Never. So what are you here for? Tell me. What have you come here for?"

Róisín felt faint, nauseous. "I just wanted to talk, to. . ." She broke out in a sweat. "Excuse me," she gasped. She rushed into the bathroom, lifted the seat and vomited a few specks of bile into the bowl. She thought she was going to be sick again and dry-retched repeatedly until her ribs hurt. "Oh God," she said. "Oh God."

She got up off the floor, turned on the cold tap, ran some water into the sink and bathed her flushed face. She put her hand out, searching like a blind person for something palpable, a purchase on life, and found the towel that Sal was holding out for her.

The two women looked at each other, burst into tears and embraced.

"I'm so sorry, Sal. I'm so sorry."

"And I didn't mean what I said, Róisín."

16

BUSINESS WAS ALWAYS SLACK mid-week and after one o'clock on Wednesday mornings the depot required just one night-rider. All the drivers took their turn. Tod usually avoided the duty, implying republican commitments, but was glad to be over his asthmatic attack and get out of the house. He was sitting in the deserted waiting room, finishing a crossword, when a drunken couple came in.

"Where are you for?" he asked.

"Where are we for?" said the man, who was tall and prematurely balding.

"Dermothill," said the woman, whose arm was linked through that of her companion.

Lovers, thought Tod. They sat in the back of his taxi, kissing and cuddling. You'd think they'd wait. He looked up at the sky and the brighter stars were just visible and he remembered Joe Powderly whose name until now had been interred with the past. Joe Powderly, who died because of sex. Or love. I got him killed. What a fucking waste. I didn't know he was in the UDR, his girlfriend told the news. I didn't know. What did it matter if he was? The poor bastard could hardly run up a street.

The lights were green and he indicated to turn into Dermothill.

"Over here. Last house on the right," said the woman. Tod slowed to a halt in the deserted street. He turned on the courtesy light. "That'll be, eh, one twenty, please," he said.

The man sat forward, switched off the light, swung his arm around Tod's neck, gripping it in a vice, almost pulling his head from its roots. Tod felt the cold metal of a gun pressed into his neck. He heard the hammer being cocked.

"Okay, Malone, do as I fucking say. Do you understand?"

Tod nodded as best he could. His heart pounded against the walls of his chest.

The woman opened the back door, got out and took the front passenger seat. She produced a small pistol. "Drive on up the mountain." Tod put the car in gear and moved off. Turning to her confederate, the woman said, "That's the others behind us now."

Tod stole a glance in his mirror and saw the lights of another car flicker up and down as the vehicles bounced over potholes on the steep mountain road.

"You know where to turn, I'm sure," he was told when they reached the top of the lane. "Reverse here."

The car which was following them, drove on a little, then stopped. Two men got out. The woman rolled down her window.

"You got him?" said a voice from the darkness.

"We got him," she laughed. "Roll down your window, Thomas."

The grip around his neck was relaxed and he did as he was told. A man bent down to address him. He could smell his aftershave, so incongruous up here among the wild smells of gorse, heather and elderberry. "Listen to this, Thomas," he said. He stuck a small tape recorder through the open window and played it. It lasted just a minute. "I couldn't believe it. Couldn't believe our luck. Do you know whose voice that is? We do."

They all laughed. He was completely crushed.

"Well?"

Tod sat outside the depot, leaning on the sill, watching two young boys on the footpath across the street playing with toy cars. The sun was still bright in the evening sky but a chill ran through the air. One of the boys opened a paper bag, took out a sweet and gave it to his companion. Neither of them spoke as they played, just made noises of engines revving and tyres braking.

"You're better!"

"Ye-yes." The appearance of Bobby had taken him by surprise.

"Are you sure you're okay?" asked Bobby.

"Still a bit shaky, them asthmatic attacks, but I couldn't lie in bed any longer."

"Is this your first night back?"

"Second. I was out on Wednesday, felt bad the last two nights and stayed in, but am out again."

"Have you seen Raymond yet?"

"No, but I will."

"You'll not get him until Monday. We're looking at something big tonight. In the early hours. Top secret. Three Branchmen. From England. I'll have to be heading. We've to be in the jump-off house right 'n' early."

"Do you want me to run you somewhere? I think there's going to be a downpour."

"No chance, it's a lovely evening. Besides, it's not far."

"Be careful," said Tod.

"You know me," said Bobby.

"Bobby!" he shouted.

The big man turned back.

"Bobby, don't mention that you saw me. I want to get another night's work out of it before Raymond puts me back in the trenches."

Bobby laughed. "I know what you mean about him. No problem!"

As he watched Bobby walk down the street Tod was inexplicably subject to confusing emotions. He felt he should be alongside Bobby and Raymond, shouldering responsibility, sharing the danger. They always said he was the best driver they had. Suddenly, he didn't know how to view things: what was right or wrong, what was true or false. There were so many perspectives. There were so many ways of living. Thinking it all out drove him demented.

He remembered how distant he found IRA Volunteers in his own district years before. They had been aloof, proud, arrogant. You couldn't understand their jokes; although, later, when he became involved he joined fully in, and enjoyed, the banter. As Bobby made his way past the post office and the hairdressers Tod observed with increasing resentment the growing distance between them. He observed Bobby's firm pace as if it was part of some secret, particular pattern from which he was now permanently excluded. In his new state he became convinced just how correct his initial opinion of republicans had been, except now they swaggered even more.

17

"Armagh Jail, 4 Oct. '84. To Raymond or Pat.
Cara, I'm bypassing normal channels and getting this to you straight through my visitor. Tod's the informer. He's a bastard. There's absolutely no doubt about it in my mind. When I was being questioned in C/Reagh the Branch had files in front of them, you know the ones about sightings and associates. Some bigwig came to the door and for a few seconds I was able to run my eyes down the page. My file was upside down but it said, 'Dance. Ardoyne. Mid-July. With Gerry Kerr.' Gerry Kerr and his brother Seamus are our people, as you know. Gerry's been in jail twice. But it was Seamus I was meeting because I had a message for him. Gerry wasn't there at all. Tod saw us. When Seamus went to the toilet or the bar Tod came over half-blocked and asked me was I seeing 'Gerry'! He obviously doesn't know which is which though there's quare differences between them. He's a fucking bastard. I have felt it in my bones that something was wrong or up with him. I don't know when exactly he became a tout but certainly after Bobby's death he was drinking and partying a lot as if he couldn't live in the present. Tod's the culprit, okay. I've no doubt. – Tina."

Squeaky came back. Tod heard him say that all was clear, as far as he could see.

Boss and Seamus Kerr left first, via the front. Squeaky and Pat were to stay behind and tidy up the house. Pat went downstairs to ask the family to keep out of the way for a minute.

Raymond put his hand on Tod's shoulders from behind as they came down the stairs. "Watch. There's a child's toy on the left." He walked Tod through the hall, avoided the closed door to the living room where the family were and went into the kitchen.

At the door into the small back garden Pat said, "I'll see you at the other end, okay?"

"Okay," replied Raymond. He had major reservations about moving Tod during daylight hours but they had little choice and they had only a short distance to travel through back entries. The heavy rain had driven most people indoors. He heard the purring of military jeeps in the distance. Then a low-flying helicopter shot across the roofs and Tod and he instinctively ducked.

In blindness, Tod walked and stumbled, with his hands tied firmly behind his back. He wasn't sure if they were telling the truth, if he was really going to another interrogation because of the threat of a raid, though he could discern military activity in the background and the helicopter was proof that they would keep a lookout for him and search for him, as promised, should the IRA pick him up. He kept getting his *theys* mixed up, just as he was repeatedly confused before about what side he was on at particular times.

What was happening to him wasn't fair. He had had no choice, otherwise he would have done something different. Had he been able to tell his story, about the way his fortunes suddenly and completely changed, that it could have happened to almost anyone; about the fear he felt; about the disgrace he prevented coming into the open; then they might have understood. But he couldn't tell and was determined not to, having already done enough damage. He made himself sound noble, acquitted himself and judged that he still had the right to live.

His admissions to his captors had been a grave, possibly fatal error. Without them he could have probably bluffed his way and discounted any allegations against him because at the end of the day he was sure that there was no proof, no evidence, only suspicion. Then he would have been up and away. He would have been free. He would have finally taken flight and taken no more chances.

The cold, wet ground beneath his bare feet was paved and he tried to imagine his surroundings. Occasionally, he limped, slowed down, took every second of life that was available to him in the hope that something would turn up. He had felt a long hedge to his left, indicating that the alley was straight. He needed the presence of a person or people to compromise Raymond. But all he could hear was rain, beating down, drumming out the entire universe.

Then he got the chance.

He heard a voice in front of them.

Raymond saw the two men in anoraks at the top of the entry. They had come from nowhere. They raised their revolvers and one shouted.

"Down on the ground! Down on the ground!"

Tod knew them to be his saviors. He immediately broke away from Raymond's grip, ducked, and ran blind towards them with all the energy in his body.

Raymond pulled out his gun and kept firing at Tod until he saw him stagger, kept firing until Tod fell into a pool of water. Raymond turned to run back the way he had come but it was too late.

18

AT FIRST TOD HADN'T BEEN SURE. Her hair was different. That's what had thrown him. He had slowed down and looked through the side window at the stumbling figure on the footpath.

Jesus Christ, he thought. What's she doing in that state? She appeared to be talking to herself and laughing. He pulled up, some yards in front, alighted from his car and hailed her.

"Tod! Tod!" she answered. "What about you. Where were you? At the disco? Was I talking to you at the disco?"

"No, I was taxiing. Do you think all I do is dance! Come on, I'll run you home."

"Are you my guardian angel now?"

"Yeah, I'm your guardian angel," he said. "Come on. In here." He held her hand as she got in. His fingers tingled with hers.

They drove off.

The smell of pub smoke cheapened her and detracted slightly from his elevated image of her, but then she smiled at him.

"Just drive a bit, Tod. I need company." She smiled again and he was flushed with pleasure, just being near her. "I don't want to go home."

"That's right, he's not due back to the morning."

"Tod, can I tell you something?"

"Is it a secret?" he joked.

"Right now, nobody else knows . . . Tod, I'm such a fraud and cheat. . ." She looked at him forthrightly as she spoke.

Jesus! She's slept with someone, he thought.

"Can I tell you? Can I?"

She was speaking fairly rationally and he wasn't as certain as he had been initially of her intoxication, even though he'd seen her lurch with his own eyes.

"Sure you can. I can keep a secret."

"Turn here, Tod."

"Here?"

"Yes, up here."

"Oh, I know where you mean now."

"Ha! You've been up here before then," she said, boldly.

He couldn't get over her freedom of speech and he simply smiled at her innuendo. At the top of the mountain lane he began reversing the car into a rutted siding covered by tall elderberry bushes then in bloom, but stopped when he saw a goat which refused to move. It stood on its hind legs, its head stretched to reach the uppermost sweet blossom. Still, the car was out of sight. Through the main arteries of the city below, the luminous bacilli of traffic silently meandered, sometimes shunted.

In one continuous outpouring she told Tod about failing her exams, that the results were humiliating and how she'd hit her son and lied and deceived her parents and friends. About how much she had drunk. Then she began sniffling.

"You poor thing," he said. "You poor thing." He noticed that she had had her hair cut. Before, her hair had cascaded around her shoulders, but now its ends fell across her cheeks and he folded it back. He took out a tissue and dabbed her face. "Easy, easy, or you'll have me covered in make-up," he joked.

"What do you advise?" she said.

"Do you not feel better now that you've told someone?"

"Yes, yes I do." She still slurred a little.

"Well, in the morning go see your parents and tell them exactly what you told me about how humiliated you felt. They'll understand. It's as simple as that. God almighty, when you think of all the pressure you've been under, it's understandable. Then phone your college friends, although from what you said they're not all that close to you so you might be able to say that you are simply repeating because you want As or Ones or something like that."

"You're right, Tod! You're absolutely right. I feel better already." She started laughing, was over-animated, as if the alcohol rekindled a joyous flame. "I'm glad I spoke to you. You're so good." She leaned forward and gave him a peck on the cheek. "I don't believe it! Do I see you blushing!"

It was impossible to see clearly in the poor light but he had turned red. He could now faintly smell her perfume or her natural scent.

With her finger she traced the whorl of his ear. "Are you embarrassed? Did you blush?"

"Probably. You're a beautiful girl, Róisín."

"'Girl!'" she laughed. "I wish I was! And 'beautiful!'"

"But you are!" he said, suggesting almost a confession of long admiration.

"You're very sweet. I've always thought it." She leaned forward to peck him again.

Just at that instant of contact he turned towards her to say something but her lips brushed across his cheek and their lips met. He kissed her and then panicked in case she misread his intentions. But she responded. Beautiful, he thought. He felt as if he were dreaming, it was so good, like something you've waited for all your life, only for the pleasure to exceed all expectations. There was a lightness about her lips, a magical dreamspeak. The first time he had been introduced to her she had struck him as being sensuous and intelligent. He stole into her bedroom once when babysitting – while Sal was downstairs – and looked around and picked up her worn clothes. He remembered the time he'd discovered her in her dressing gown, fixing the sink, when Raymond was still in jail, and how he'd admired and desired her.

He opened his mouth a little and her tongue entered and he clammed it between his lips. Then he opened her shirt and with his thumb he felt for the stud of her nipple underneath her bra. At first her elbow resisted him and he feared the embarrassment of rejection but then her fingers played with his nape and neck and inside his jacket and across his stomach. She kissed him like someone who had been deprived of passion. Then they both hesitated. Slowed down. Stopped.

"Whow-ee," she said, controlling her breathing and running both hands down her cheeks.

"Ahem," said Tod, a gesture to concur with her own resumption of proper behavior. "Yes," he said. "Well." They both nervously laughed. Said nothing. Looked at each other. Her shirt was still lying open. Then Tod thought, you're only on earth once. He yearned for her and within three or four seconds the protocol had dissolved and he kissed her all over the face and she responded in part. But Tod forgot about the future, about tomorrow, about other people, and, unaware, he overtook even her and tumbled through the weightless universe of sex, not hearing Róisín mumble, "Tod, no. Please. No, Tod;" faintly hearing the goat knocking at the window and the rap dulling his pleasure so that he tightened his eyes, excluded the real world and surged on through the supreme darkness. The window was rapped again, this time harder, and Tod was back on earth with a jolt and his heart rose in his throat as he heard the English accent laugh.

"Want a hand, mate!"

"Jesus Christ. Aw Jesus, Jesus, Jesus," whispered Tod, as beads of sweat swarmed like lice up through the raised hair on

his head. Their car was surrounded by soldiers. Róisín panicked, threw Tod off, pulled up her briefs and burst into tears.

Tod tucked himself in and pulled up his trousers to make
himself presentable. The soldier tried the handle of the door.
The door opened. He peered in. In his hand he held a small
tape recorder, to save him having to write down details. "Don't
be upset, darlin'. Didn't you enjoy it? Don't worry, we won't
keep you a minute . . . Any longer than he did! . . . Name, sir?"

"Ah, Thomas Malone."

"Speak up, sir."

"Thomas Malone."

"Howdya spell it, please?"

"Thomas?"

"No," the soldier laughed. "Macarown or whatever it was.
Your surname."

"MALONE."

"Could I see your driver's license?"

Another soldier came over. Streaks of camouflage cream on
his face made him look savage and Róisín found his silence
menacing. She began to shake.

Tod had removed his license from behind the shade and
handed it over. The soldier spoke the details into the tape.

"And yours, darlin'?"

Róisín didn't know from where came her answer. "Sal. Sal
Malone."

"Speak up, please."

"Sal Malone."

"You related then?"

"She's my wife," said Tod.

"For feck's sake, we thought we'd caught you with somebody else's!" laughed the soldier.

"And date of birth, darlin'?"

"Eh, nineteenth of the sixth, sixty-five."

"And that's all there is to it. Simple, wasn't it," said the soldier. "And some people complain of harassment! Sorry to

have bothered you. You can carry on. . ." he said, with a grin. "Good night."

"Good night," said Tod. The sweat on his back had coagulated into a vest of salt which hurt like sunburn when he moved. Róisín was still shaking. "It's okay," he said. "It's okay. They're new into the area. Didn't recognize me. Are you alright? Are you?"

She nodded, yes.

"Róisín, please don't tell Raymond. He'd kill me if he ever found out."

She sat glum, staring down into her fingers which counted invisible beads. He was amazed at how sober a drunk person could be.

"Róisín . . . Róisín! Please don't tell Raymond, won't you not?"

"Let's go, Tod. Please, let's get out of here. I have to go to the bathroom."

"No, let's wait a minute, in case they're still down the lane." There was an awkward silence. "Róisín, what date of birth did you give. Can you remember?"

"I just made it up. I can't remember what it was." She delivered her replies without looking him in the face.

"I don't think they know Sal's, so that's okay. Róisín, are you listening to me? Don't tell Raymond. Whatever you do, don't tell."

She sighed. "I won't tell him. I won't tell him."

"Thank God for that . . . Róisín, I am sorry. I don't know what came over me. I thought you wanted to do it. And then I was in a world of my own."

"It's not your fault, Tod, and it's not my fault. But what's done is done. Now, let's go."

The journey home was made in complete silence, as if between two people who despised each other. At times he thought she was asleep, but when he looked across he saw that she was in a daze.

She got out of the car a discreet distance from her corner.

"You okay?" he shouted.

"I will be," she said. It was the first time she had looked at him. It was the face of decency destroyed. Within the shell of the car Tod felt very, very small.

"Let's just never mention this again. To any one," she said, firmly.

"You're right," he said. "Night night."

"Night night," she replied, but both knew their relationship was changed utterly.

As he drove off, he rolled the window down further and gulped in fresh air, as if the state of his soul could be so easily laundered and fate so easily outwitted. He knew he could trust her. She would not say anything. That was one of her strengths – to be dignified: to bear pain or loss, or guilt even, in silence. And as he drew some comfort in having survived yet another close shave he smiled and his complacency grew. But then, something within him revolted as if he'd reached a critical point, and he became appalled at what he had done to Raymond, to Sal and Nuala, and Aidan, to his family, friends and comrades. He suddenly saw himself not in the same light that those closest to him mistakenly and indulgently saw him, but as a divinity might see him across time and into his heart – a manipulative, exploitative, egotistical individual who had squandered nobility.

Tod drowned in shame. He pulled the car over and gripped the steering wheel, gasping for air. He used his inhaler like a junky and then began to cry and bang his head off the steering wheel. He wanted to make up for everything, to pay for his wrongs. And he saw more wrongs now across the complicated landscape of his recent years than unfaithfulness and lust. He saw his dead. I don't deserve to live, he thought. I should fucking hang myself from the nearest tree. He used the sleeves of his jumper to mop up his tears and calmed himself.

I swear, that's it. I've learnt my lesson. I'm sorry for all the messing about, I'm sorry about all the hurt and pain. And Sal knows. Deep down inside Sal knows what I'm at and she doesn't say a thing, not a thing, when I come creeping in in the early hours. What a bastard I've become. But that's it. God, I swear, that's it.

Tod took a deep breath of fresh air, of new life, and drove home to Sal and Nuala, imagining the beginnings of a new man.

By the same author

West Belfast

ISBN 1-57098-043-8 paper, 255 pages, $12.95

The novel opens in an innocent setting of youthfulness. Morrison creates the scene as he tells a fascinating story of love and tragedy set in the streets of war-torn Belfast. The novel records the increasing political tension and civil unrest which explodes to the foreground in 1969. The activity leading to the arrival of the British Army and afterwards is described with a vividly detailed immediacy.

John endured sectarian abuse in a Protestant factory. In the IRA, he carries out bombings and raids. He is arrested, brutally interrogated and tortured by the security forces before being jailed. Expelled from school, Angela's rebellion is within herself, often dismaying her parents. She swings between the drug scene in London and a Belfast she finds too confining.

Home life in working class Belfast of the sixties is drawn with skill and great feeling. Morrison paints lyrical and devastating word pictures in this very personal portrayal of a city that has endured much and where there still remains a divided people.

On the Back of the Swallow

ISBN 1-57098-101-9 paper, 256 pages, $14.95

This haunting novel, set in Ireland, tells of tragic loss and doomed love. Nicky Smith's best friend, Robin Coulter, dies when they are both fifteen. Later, after years of trying to find his place in the world, he meets Gareth Williams, a fifteen-year-old boy whose vulnerability and brilliance remind him of the dead Robin. A passionate friendship develops which ultimately provokes the crushing forces of a vengeful society. Nicky's harrowing time in prison is skillfully drawn.

Nicky's sexuality is portrayed variously throughout the novel. Morrison's view is that terms of sexuality cannot be restricted by society, but must be defined by the individual. *On the Back of the Swallow* breaks through misinformed opinions and demystifies homosexuality, revealing it as a warm and stable lifestyle threatened by bigotry, hatred and prejudice.

By Gerry Adams

Falls Memories: A Belfast Life

ISBN 1-879373-96-3 paper, 154 pages, $10.95

This nostalgic and very personal account of a working-class Irish community abounds with light-hearted humor.

"An interesting and indeed important addition to the understanding of the ingredients that coalesced to lead to the long years of violence in this part of the world." – *The Derry Journal*

The Street and Other Stories

ISBN 1-57098-132-9 paper, 160 pages, $12.95

". . . serious art. It is a good bet that James Joyce would read Gerry Adams' short stories to learn about souls in Belfast as the world reads *Dubliners*." – James F. Clarity, *New York Times* writer, in the *Sunday Independent*

"Sinn Féin President Gerry Adams is a natural storyteller." – *Irish Echo*

"He writes convincingly and with compassion. . . The warmth of Adams' writing comes from the affection of a man for the remembered things of his past." – *Times Literary Supplement*

Cage Eleven

ISBN 1-57098-131-0 paper, 160 pages, $12.95

Gerry Adams was interned without trial in Long Kesh prison during the 1970s. This is his own passionate and humorous account of the daily struggles in Long Kesh, and of his fellow prisoners.

"Quite brilliant . . . a tribute to a particular kind of survival, by a group of people who have committed their lives to a deeply-held political belief about their country. . ." – *Books Ireland*

Free Ireland: Towards a Lasting Peace

ISBN 1-879373-95-5 paper, 240 pages, $11.95

Adams' powerful statement on the meaning, importance and inspiration of modern Irish republicanism.

"One corrective. . . to the flow of misinformation that passes for journalistic analysis of affairs in the North of Ireland, both in Britain and the Republic." – *New Statesman*

By Tim Pat Coogan

Michael Collins: The Man Who Made Ireland

ISBN 1-57098-075-6 paper, 480 pages, $16.95

The story of a man who became a legend in his own lifetime, and who was later assassinated by partisans who felt he had betrayed them.

"Superb. . . this will be a hard Life to beat." – *The Times Literary Supplement*

*Over 300,000 sold

The IRA: A History

ISBN 1-879373-99-8 paper, 542 pages, $18.95

The historical background of the Irish struggles, including extensive interviews with figures from both sides of the sectarian divide.

". . . the standard reference work on the subject. . ." – *The New York Times*

"No student of Irish history can afford to ignore this book. No scholar is likely to improve upon it. . . A fascinating book, of the greatest possible value to us all." – *The Times Literary Supplement*

* Over 250,000 sold

The Troubles: Ireland's Ordeal 1966–1996 and the Search for Peace

ISBN 1-57098-092-6 cloth $29.95,
1-57098-144-2 paper, $18.95, 488 pages

Using never before published information, the author studies this deep conflict involving the politics of Britain, Ireland, and America.

"Coogan fills his book with quotes, personal reportage, and wry wit. . . This title should be part of any history or current events collection." - *Library Journal*

By Bobby Sands

Writings from Prison

ISBN 1-57098-113-2 paper, 240 pages, $12.95

Bobby Sands was an IRA prisoner who led a fatal hunger strike that brought the plight of the Catholics in Northern Ireland to the attention of the world. While behind bars, he secretly wrote two books, concealing them until they were smuggled out; both are here collected under one cover. With dry humor, *One Day in My Life* charts a man's attempt to preserve his identity against cold, dirt and boredom. In *Skylark Sing Your Lovely Song*, Sands tells in prose and verse of the struggle that won him fame throughout the world.

To order any of the above please call the toll free number or order from the address below. Send payment with order (check, VISA, Mastercard) and include $3 for postage and handling for each order.

Roberts Rinehart publishes a number of titles of Irish interest. To receive further information and to be put on our mailing list, please write to us or telephone the toll free number below.

Roberts Rinehart Publishers
5455 Spine Road, Mezzanine West
Boulder, Colorado 80301
1 800 352 1985